Christmas at Belhaven Hall

Christmas at Belhaven Hall

A Maidens of Marbury Romance

Karla Kratovil

Christmas at Belhaven Hall

Tule Publishing First Printing, October 2022

The Tule Publishing, Inc.

First Publication by Tule Publishing 2022

Cover design by Erin Dameron-Hill

ISBN: 978-1-958686-31-7

Dedication

To my gift wrapping, tree chopping, carol singing, eggnog making purveyor of all holiday cheer, I love you.

Prologue

September 1826

MAXWELL DRAKE LAY staring up at the blanket of stars above him and groaned. He tried to suck in a breath of humid air, but the searing pain that tore through his side froze the breath in his lungs. Had the stiletto Gus stabbed him with punctured a lung? He slid a hand slowly up to his left side and gently probed the spot. His fingers gleamed wet and red in the moonlight. His right shoulder throbbed, and he tried to move his arm to a more comfortable position, but it refused. It had to be dislocated. He cursed through swollen lips.

The night had started out promising, with plans to attend a masquerade party at Duka del Loredan's grand house. The party always included fine wine and beautiful women, and tonight, a concrete deal for the Vasari. That painting would have made him enough to pay off his bills and travel to Paris to visit his mother and sisters. He was done with this city. He gritted his teeth through another sharp blaze of pain as he breathed in and out. It appeared Venice was done with him as well.

He experimentally stretched his legs, bending each at the knee and carefully rotating each ankle. Everything worked; nothing seemed broken. However, the bruises would no doubt ache by morning if he lived that long. He blinked rapidly as the stars went blurry with tears. He tried to lever himself to a seated position with his good arm, but the movement caused a tearing sensation in his left side, and he fell back to the street with an anguished cry. Then, breathing carefully through his nose, he concentrated on the sky. A long thin cloud blew across the stars like a wispy wraith.

Max sent up a prayer to the heavens. *Please, God, don't let me die here in the gutter. If you deign to save my life, I promise to turn over a new leaf. I will go straight and find a respectable job, love my neighbor, and all that. Just give me a chance. I can turn my life around.*

He lay there for a long time, still as a corpse. Perhaps God didn't listen to the prayers of thieves and charlatans. Then a whistle blew into the night, two short and two long blasts. Max gathered all his waning strength, and using his good arm, he raised it into the air, ignoring the pain. "I'm here, Assan," he called out.

Four days later

MAX CRACKED HIS eyes open slowly. Sunshine streamed through a window and seared his eyeballs. He closed the lids and flung his right arm over his eyes. Searing pain raced up his side, and he yelped at its burn.

"Don't move too much, my friend. You are barely alive as it is." Assan's gravelly voice came from across the room.

Max cracked his eyelids again and dared to turn his head toward the sound. Assan sat in a chair, with one ankle crossed over the other knee and a newspaper in his lap. They were in a strange bedroom, the dark wood walls and green velvet-covered furnishing unfamiliar. Max tried to speak, but his mouth felt stuffed with cotton. He darted his tongue out to lick his cracked lips.

Assan stood and crossed to the nightstand and poured a cup of water. He brought it carefully to Max's lips. Max drank greedily and immediately felt better. "Thank you, my friend, for finding me. For saving my life."

Assan nodded his head; his dark eyes were solemn. "We are even."

Max nodded in return. Five years ago, he had saved Assan from a blood-thirsty mob at an open market in Cairo. Somehow Assan had accidentally insulted one of the dealers. Asking poorly in Sa'idi to purchase the man's daughter when he actually wanted to purchase a gold watch. They were indeed even. "Can you help me sit up, please?"

His friend frowned. "Are you sure?" At Max's nod, Assan slipped his hands under his armpits and hefted Max up to lean against the headboard. Then he piled two pillows behind his back. It hurt, especially under his right arm, but Max felt much improved sitting upright. He looked down, long coils of white linen strip wrapped around his chest. "I was sure he had punctured my lung with that blade."

"The surgeon said you were fortunate," Assan replied. "Whose blade?"

"Gus and his gang of thugs." Max ran a hand down over his face. "They ambushed me on the way to the party. There were too many of them to fight off."

"Gustav Benelli is a dangerous enemy. He has been jealous of you ever since the Finola deal. Will you go to the polizia?"

"And what? Tell them that the stolen painting I procured for the Duka del Loredan was stolen from me? Do you think the Duka will vouch for me?" Max shook his head. The powerful elite didn't muddy their hands with the politics of the underworld. No doubt, Benelli had already sold the painting to Loredan. The Duka only cared that he received the item he wanted, not who sold it to him. Max leaned his head back and closed his eyes. He was so tired.

"Would you like something to eat? You have been subsisting on broth while you were in and out of your fever."

Max opened his eyes. "Yes, please." His stomach growled loudly in response, making Assan chuckle. His friend went over to ring the bell for a servant. "Where are we?"

"My father's home."

Max grimaced. "Thank you again. I know how hard it is for you to deal with your family."

"I couldn't take you back to your house." Assan shrugged. "Plus, you needed a surgeon. When my father calls for a surgeon, everyone scrambles to do his bidding."

A knock at the door pulled their attention away from the delicate subject of Assan's family. A maid stepped through the doorway with a tray of food. The smell of cumin, cinnamon, and meat reached Max's nose. His stomach let out another loud rumble. Assan took the tray from her, and she shuffled back out of the room.

"My mother insisted they have something hot ready for you when you woke. She says this stew feeds the blood. Trust me; you need it."

Once the tray was set on his lap, Max wasted no time tucking into the bowl of stew. His shoulder ached, but the pain did not deter him from the delicious food.

Assan sat in the chair he had previously occupied. He frowned. "I went to your house. The entire place had been ransacked. That is why I was out looking for you."

"Goddammit," Max exclaimed around a mouthful of food.

"Your housekeeper wasn't home; she was visiting with her sister."

Max nodded. "I gave her the night off."

"I went back yesterday, and she had already put the house to rights. She gave me some clothes for you and a stack of correspondence that arrived a couple of days ago." Assan stood and went over to the desk to retrieve a stack of mail. "You're welcome. I've become your errand boy."

Max grinned at his friend's sour expression. He'd finished eating and exchanged the food tray for his mail. Funny that his housekeeper had thought to send it to him, you'd think that reading his correspondence could have waited until after he wasn't mostly dead. The first letter on the top was from his mother. Ah, well, that explained it. Signora Rossi believed family was of the utmost importance. He flipped past the letter and through several more when one caught his eye. The return address was London, Knightsbridge & Sons. He sliced the seal open with his thumb and unfolded the parchment. It was dated three months ago.

Dear Mr. Drake,

We must impart the sad news that your cousin, the Earl of Rivenhall, passed away on the tenth of December. We have had some difficulty ascertaining your whereabouts, which is why this missive is delayed in reaching you with this terrible news. You are the next line to inherit. Please respond immediately with the date of your planned return to England. Your presence is required for the inheritance and entailment to be properly transferred.

Yours sincerely,
Alfred P. Knightsbridge

"You look as though you have seen a ghost." Assan looked over with concern.

Max shook his head. "I have. My cousin Henry died last December. They had trouble reaching me."

"I'm sorry to hear your news, my friend."

Max stared down at the words on the page, shock melting into sorrow. Henry was dead? How could this be? The message was annoyingly brief, lacking in any details about what had happened to his cousin. The message began to sink in. *You are the next line to inherit.* He took a deep breath in then hissed at the sharp pain that tore through his side. How could he be the next earl? He could never fill Henry's shoes. His thoughts raced back to the other night, the fight, the beating, lying in that street bleeding, gasping for breath. He closed his eyes. What had he become?

Six years ago, he had left behind his job at the Louvre to join his father dealing in stolen art and artifacts. Father had pressured him to come into the business, and Max, feeling betrayed and angry by the woman he'd loved, had thrown all his carefully laid plans aside. He ran a hand down over his face and looked again at the letter in his lap.

Henry's heir. A chance to start over. A chance to be someone different, respectable. His desperate prayer to live another day had been answered. In return, he owed God a promise to be a better man.

Chapter One

December 10, 1826

MAX PULLED DOWN the brim of his wool hat, trying in vain to keep the stinging droplets of icy rain out of his eyes. Damn, had the weather always been so bloody miserable in early December? Or had he become spoiled by the warm Mediterranean climate? He was freezing his bollocks off in this wind. His horse nickered in agreement blowing out a stream of warm breath visible in the freezing air. "We are almost there, boy." He patted the horse on its wet neck. "At least I think we are." Max peered through the late afternoon gloom trying to get his bearings and remember the turn to reach Belhaven Hall.

Eight years had passed since he had last been at his cousin's house. Memories of that last sun-drenched summer lay crisp and clear in his mind. Lazy mornings fishing in the river, racing at breakneck speed across the fields, laughter and teasing banter flung back and forth between him and his best friends. The three of them had been inseparable; Henry, Livvy, and him. And the day he had finally gotten the courage to kiss Livvy, well, his whole world had tilted in those stolen moments in the orchard. Max shook his head at the foolish boy he had been at eighteen. How he'd believed he could conquer the world and that love held constancy.

He hunched his shoulders trying to burrow deeper into his greatcoat and was grateful to his grandmother for insisting on outfitting him with winter wardrobe essentials before leaving Paris. He had spent less than a week in London before hiring a horse to make the trip to Herefordshire. At the meeting with the solicitor to go over the details of Henry's will and sign all the papers to take possession of the entail officially, Max had received a slim envelope. When he cut open the seal, inside, there were three letters. One letter with his name, one addressed to Olivia, and one addressed to Julien. Who was Julien?

The solicitor had been a starchy fellow, older than God himself. The man's white bushy eyebrows lowered when Max asked why the letters had not been given to Lady Rivenhall and the other person. "The letters belong to you, my lord. The contents of the envelope were left to the next Lord Rivenhall. It would not be my place to open a sealed folder."

Max ran a finger over Olivia's name scrawled across the letter. This message from her husband had languished in this envelope for a whole year. He had decided to leave the next day for Belhaven. She deserved to have her letter.

Henry dead. Somehow it seemed impossible that cheerful, clever Henry was no longer on this earth. As hurt as Max had been when he heard the news of Henry and Olivia's marriage, he never wished for this, one friend dead and the other a widow far too young.

Tightening his hands on the reins, he guided his horse around a large puddle. Perhaps he should have stayed the night at the inn instead of heading out on horseback. But once he had made it to Marbury, he just wanted to finish this last leg to Belhaven Hall. It had been a long day of traveling. A fresh horse and the promise that his trunk would be delivered tomorrow was all that was needed to convince him to travel the last bit. What should have taken an hour at most had turned into double that as his horse slogged through the cold rain-soaked countryside.

Finally, the iron gates that stood sentry at the entrance to Belhaven Hall's park appeared. Max paused and wiped the rain from his face. Despite the coating of ice on everything, the place was familiar as ever. Tall oak and aspen trees filled the grounds, their bare branches reaching out to arch over the drive. Nudging his horse to walk they made their way toward the large medieval manor looming in the distance. The manor sat on a hill; four stone turrets marked the old stronghold section which had been built in 1545. Two more turrets flanked a massive stone archway, marking the more modern manor entrance in front. Its great wooden doors soared at least fifteen feet. Built by Henry's grandfather, the architect he hired had seamlessly integrated the stone façade to match the older section, thus preserving the effect of a medieval castle.

The thought that Olivia lived alone in this ancient house

with all its ghosts made him inexplicably angry. *How dare Henry die on her?* Of course, the more pressing question was what was Max going to do about her? He frowned at the house as he pulled his horse to a stop in front. As the new earl, it would hardly be proper to have his predecessor's widow living in the house. His heart raced in his chest. What would Livvy be like eight years later? At seventeen, she had been a delicate beauty with porcelain skin and thick golden hair, long legs that made her hard to beat in a foot race, and wide brown eyes that were often wary but would sparkle with good humor when he made her laugh. And he had made it his mission to make her laugh, his antics more and more ridiculous just to see her smile widen and hear the rich tone of her mirth.

He pulled his thoughts from the past. He was here to settle things with his cousin's widow. Perhaps she would like to have a townhouse in London. There she could be part of society and find a new husband. He also needed to get the new estate manager he'd hired settled. Max knew next to nothing about running an estate this size. He never intended to have this role. He dismounted and approached the bell pull, and the rain was coming down in earnest now. He waited impatiently for the door to open. When no one answered, he pulled it again. Nothing.

Max reached for the door handle and, turning the large brass knob, he pushed the door open. The entrance hall was empty. He turned and shut the door behind him before pulling off his soaking wet hat. Where were the bloody servants? A young woman in a maid's uniform came around the corner from the left-wing. She skidded to a stop when she spotted him and let out a high-pitched squeak. She clutched a vase that held a bouquet of holly berries and greenery to her chest. Then she executed the sign of the cross before turning on her heel and rushing away.

What the hell?

Max ran a hand through his hair to slick the wet locks away from his forehead. "Hello! Anybody here?" he called out.

In the next moment, an older man rushed into the hall, the maid at his elbow. "Now, Enid, I have told you that there is no such thing as ghosts a hundred times. See, a flesh-and-blood man." The servant approached. "I apologize, sir. What a terrible night to be traveling. How may I help you?"

"I am Maxwell Drake. I believe I was expected."

The man's mouth opened and closed. "Lord Rivenhall! I am Mr. Daniels, the butler. Welcome, welcome. We were not expecting you until tomorrow. John, who is usually at the door, is ill. Oh, dear. Let me take your coat."

The poor man was so flustered Max's annoyance at having to let himself into his own house dissipated. "It's all right. I did plan to arrive tomorrow but was eager to finish the journey, so I pushed through from Marbury this afternoon." He handed his greatcoat to Mr. Daniels. "Is Lady Rivenhall at home?"

"Yes, right this way."

Max followed the butler to the right, down a corridor lit

with sconces. The butler opened the fourth door and stepped inside to announce him. Max waited in the doorway and scanned the space. A pretty drawing room with creamy yellow walls and white moldings. Large windows along one wall framed the gloomy landscape outside. Across the room, a settee faced a large fireplace where a cheerful fire roared. And there she was. Her profile was achingly familiar even after so many years. Olivia sat facing a man with dark curly hair and a chiseled jawline. The two were deep in conversation. Then she leaned forward, and the man embraced her in a long hug.

"Pardon me, madam," the butler approached the two. "You have a guest. Lord Rivenhall has arrived."

Olivia jumped to her feet, her expression one of guilty surprise. And no wonder, after being caught in an embrace with her lover. The stab of jealousy was sharp in his gut and utterly ridiculous. Lady Rivenhall was a widow of almost a year; she could take any lover she wanted. Of course, someone with her beauty would not be pining away alone.

He cleared his throat. "Please don't let me interrupt."

Chapter Two

MAXWELL DRAKE FILLED the doorway. His hair was wet from the weather, and his expression enigmatic. Her memories of him were of a tall, lanky boy with a smile that would split his face open. This man in front of her looked stern and forbidding. His boyish features replaced by sharp cheekbones and jawline carved from granite. His eyes narrowed, and his lips curved up in a thin wry smile as he stared at her. Olivia's heart raced in her chest at seeing him again.

"Max, I mean, Mr. Drake." Olivia shook her head, trying to gather her scattered wits. "I mean, Lord Rivenhall, what a surprise. We were not expecting you until tomorrow." She walked around the settee to give herself a moment to gather her composure. But the closer she got to him, the more details she noticed, like the breadth of his shoulders under his fine wool jacket and the golden hue of his suntanned skin. His amber-colored eyes roamed over her as she approached, assessing her as she did him, perhaps looking for the similarities to the adolescent selves who had known each other so well.

She paused before him, tilting her chin up to meet his

gaze. Although his expression was carefully neutral and his posture stiff, his eyes blazed with a wild gleam that reminded her of the boy she'd known. She gave him a tentative smile. "Welcome home, Max."

"It's good to see you, Livvy. I'm so sorry for your loss. I didn't know about Henry until just two months ago."

Olivia wrapped her arms around her waist. Anger flickered like a small flame in her chest. "Yes, well, I guess when you are off traveling the world, it's hard to keep up with your correspondence." Max's eyes widened at her sharp comment, but she didn't regret it. Max had broken promises and turned his back on friends, turned his back on her. She faced Julien. "Please let me introduce you to Mr. Galey, he was a dear friend of Henry's. Mr. Galey, this is the new Lord Rivenhall."

Julien stood and gave a slight bow. "Welcome, Lord Rivenhall." He smiled sadly. "That is going to take some getting used to."

Max nodded. "You and me both. Please call me Drake."

Olivia held out a hand to Julien, so grateful to have someone to share her grief with. They had each loved Henry in different ways and forged a strong bond of friendship in the last year. He gave her hand a brief squeeze.

"I think I will go find a book from the library. I'll see you both at dinner." Julien headed for the door.

Olivia turned back to Max, and she almost took a step back, his dark eyebrows were pulled down, and his lips pulled into a scowl. She straightened her shoulders. "You must be chilled to the bone. Can I offer you anything? A brandy? A hot toddy, perhaps?"

"A brandy sounds good," Max replied.

Olivia walked over to the sidebar and poured two glasses. A brandy sounded like just the thing to burn away the shock of seeing Maxwell Drake again. Ever since she had received the letter from the solicitor that he would be arriving this week, her stomach had been in knots. She'd told herself her nerves were because his arrival would mean she would actually have to leave Belhaven Hall and do something with her life; that the nerves had nothing to do with the man himself. It had been eight years since she'd seen him last. Certainly, any old feelings of puppy love she had held for him were long gone.

But the minute he walked through the door, her traitorous heart had jumped into her throat. Well, just because he was still the most gorgeous man she'd ever laid eyes on didn't mean she would turn into a puddle at his feet. He had left her behind and not returned. He didn't deserve even the smallest of fond feelings. She took in a calming breath before turning back to Max.

"Please sit down by the fire." Olivia handed him his glass.

Max sat and stretched out his long legs toward the fire. He took a sip of brandy and sighed. "This is excellent."

Olivia sat in a chair to his right. "Henry had excellent taste." She took a sip and allowed the smoky flavor to roll over her tongue. When she looked up, Max had his eyebrows raised high.

"Since when do you drink brandy?"

Olivia shrugged. Truth be told, she never drank spirits. But tonight called for something stronger than her usual glass of sherry wine. "I'm not the same girl you left behind eight years ago."

Max drank from his glass. "Yes, I suppose I am realizing that."

"Besides, tonight is the one-year anniversary of Henry's death. So, if there was ever a time to have a drink, tonight is it." She took a larger swallow. One year ago today, her safe existence had been snatched away. Henry had been her protector and her friend. She'd lived in a strange limbo in the year since, not sure where her place in the world would be now. She would not be able to stay at Belhaven unless Max approved of her idea. Even then, she would have to leave the castle. It was not her house anymore.

Max choked on his brandy. "Today?"

Olivia nodded.

"How did it happen?" Max asked.

"He was outside of London coming home from a friend's party. The wheel axle cracked when it hit a rut, and the whole carriage flipped onto its door side. The coachman was thrown from his seat and hit his head on a rock." She took a more measured sip this time. This was the worst part. "When he came to, the whole thing was engulfed in flames. There was no way to save Henry."

Max sat silent for several moments. "I'm so sorry, Livvy.

I am still trying to wrap my head around the idea that he is gone. It seems impossible."

Olivia stared into the fire. "Where have you been, Max?"

"Most recently? Italy."

Olivia turned her gaze back to him. "Italy?"

"Venice. I had been hired to track down a rare painting. My mother knew where to reach me."

"Except I didn't know where your family was either. It took months for the solicitors to track her down in Paris. And I guess months more to get the letter to you." Months that she had been on tenterhooks waiting to find out her fate. Months of mourning. The anger that had begun as a small flame in her chest spread as she thought about the uncertainty she had lived with this last year—damn Maxwell Drake for being so careless with his friendships and with her heart.

She drained the last of her brandy and set the glass down with a thump. Well, tonight certainly was not the time to present her case to the new owner of her home. She needed a clear head and all of her arguments in place to convince Max to let her continue to run the estate as his land steward. As unconventional as the notion might be, no one knew the workings of the estate better than her, and she would tell him so tomorrow. Olivia stood. "I'll have Mr. Daniels show you to your room. Dinner is at eight."

Max stood as well. "I think tonight I would prefer a hot bath and a hot meal in my room. I wouldn't make fit company for you and your friend Mr. Galey."

Olivia nodded, relieved that she would not have to endure an evening of stilted conversation. "I understand. I will see you tomorrow then." She turned to leave.

"Livvy," Max called out.

Her hand still on the door, Olivia turned. "Yes?"

Max stared at her for a long moment. His brows lowered, creating a small furrow between them. "It's nice to see you again." Then his lips curved up in a tentative smile.

Olivia's heart flipped over in her chest, and she frowned at its foolishness. "Good night, Max."

Chapter Three

MAX SQUINTED AT his reflection in the cloudy mirror as he finished tying his cravat. This morning at breakfast, he would do his best to be charming. Things had not gotten off on the right foot last night. Seeing Olivia again affected him in ways he had not expected. The moment she turned those doe eyes toward him, his wits had scrambled and sent his emotions tumbling back to the past. She looked beautiful as ever. Her soft blonde waves, which had, at seventeen, flowed wildly down her back, had been piled in a neat topknot, and her skin no longer sprinkled with freckles was instead pale as cream. The deep brown of her eyes made a startling contrast to her complexion. When she stood to greet him, he admired how her figure had filled out, her lush curves swathed in black silk.

Jealousy flooded his gut when he saw her and Mr. Galey embracing and reaching for each other's hands in silent communication. Henry's friend. *Pah!* Max snorted. How long had the man waited before slithering in to seduce her?

He crossed the deep carpet that covered the stone floors of the bedroom. Mr. Daniels had explained that this was the traditional suite for the master of the hall. It was in the older section, what used to be the original keep. According to the butler, Henry and Olivia preferred the modern wing of the house. Their suite in that section was where Lady Rivenhall still resided. Max picked up his jacket from the edge of the bed and slipped it on. This room was certainly large and imposing enough to be the lord's suite. A giant bed sat in the middle of the room, sporting deep red curtains. Two large mullioned windows flanked the bed. An enormous fireplace had kept him warm last night despite the cold drafts zipping through the room making the candles flicker.

It hadn't gotten past him that Olivia had put him on the opposite end of the house from where she slept. Or that she hadn't exactly been welcoming, with her sharp comments and her stiff good night.

Max sighed. He hadn't even realized that it was the anniversary of Henry's death. Was it any wonder she hadn't been warm and friendly? He slipped Henry's letters into his pocket. He wouldn't forget to give it to her this morning. Perhaps it would give her some peace. He left the room to find his way to breakfast.

Down the long stone corridor lined with iron sconces, the hallway intersected with another corridor. How the architect managed to merge the new structure so seamlessly with the old keep was truly amazing. Max ran a hand across the wall as it changed from stone to plaster at a rounded corner. Once through the archway, he turned left. He approached Henry's childhood room, and two doors down was the room Max had always stayed in when he visited.

Because his father had been a diplomat, their family had lived in various cities throughout the continent; Berlin, Budapest, Naples, and Cairo. Max had been happy when he was old enough to go to Eton with his cousin Henry. Too far to travel home on breaks, his parents had been in Budapest then, he had always come home with Henry during school holidays. He stopped in front of his old door.

So many happy memories were had in these hallways and rooms. When they were twelve, Henry and he had been obsessed with hunting the ghosts that purportedly haunted the Hall. They'd listened attentively to all the tales Henry's father would weave about the history of the house. And then they set out to see the ghosts for themselves.

Max laid a hand against the door. God, poor Henry. How was it possible that his life was cut so short? He was the kind of good, decent fellow that was needed more of in this world. Max's anger and resentment had created a ball of guilt that sat like a rock in the pit of his stomach. These old feelings had kept him from keeping in touch with his cousin. They had caused him to ignore Henry's letters. Now he would never have a chance to explain how he'd felt—the reason why he'd been so angry. The opportunity to repair their friendship was gone forever.

"You know, you can switch rooms if you want your old room back." Olivia's voice pierced his melancholy thoughts. He could hear the wry humor in her tone.

He slowly turned, his feelings still churning. Suddenly, he needed to know what had happened. Why had she never written back to him? How had Henry wooed her heart away? Had she been lonely? Had her feelings been so mercurial?

Olivia wore a wide smile, and her eyes gleamed with laughter. He was transported back to when he was nineteen and would have done anything to make her smile. She had been through enough this past year. Henry was dead, and the past was the past. It would do no good to rehash it now. He swallowed the lump in his throat but couldn't seem to muster a witty response. He managed a weak smile and a shrug of his shoulders.

Olivia closed the distance between them, concern replacing the laughter in her expression. "I forget that you have not had the same amount of time to get used to the idea that he is gone."

"Even receiving the letter did not prepare me for the truth of him not being here." He mustered a wry smile. "I was just thinking about our ghost-hunting days. We were determined to find and converse with the ghosts of the Hall."

Olivia's smile returned. "Well, the ghosts are still around. You may get your chance still. Here, let's go down to breakfast."

Max followed her down the curved marble stairs that led to the main entrance hall. They went left and into a small cozy morning room. Mrs. Peabody bustled through a door on the opposite side of the room. "Well, if it isn't the missing heir." Her smile bloomed. "Come here, Master Drake, and let me have a look at you."

Max dutifully crossed the room to greet the housekeeper. Besides a few laugh lines around her eyes and some gray threaded through her hair, she looked as young and vital as ever. He bent to buss her cheek. "Good morning Mrs. Peabody. It's lovely to see you again."

She stepped back and looked him up and down. "You've grown into a fine specimen of a man. Look how suntanned you are! Where have you been?"

"Italy."

She placed a hand to her chest. "Oh my! How exotic. Now I hope you won't be disappointed in our old-fashioned English breakfast."

"Mrs. Peabody, you can't imagine how much I have missed an English breakfast. Do you still make those delicious honey cakes?"

"Of course! I remember they were your favorite."

Olivia stepped forward and gestured to the small round table. "Let's sit. I remember your affinity for honey as well. You know, we still keep beehives on the western edge of the gardens."

"Do you?" Max pulled out a chair for Olivia. "There is nothing as good as fresh honey."

Mrs. Peabody left through the door she had entered, and Max rounded the table to sit down opposite Olivia.

She delicately blew on her hot tea. "I'd be happy to take you around the property. It's not raining, and the air is fresh and crisp this morning." Olivia took a sip of tea and glanced across the table. "There is not much happening now, but I can fill you in on plans for this spring."

"The solicitor informed me that your father is no longer in his position. He said no new land steward had been hired and that Henry had been handling things himself. The man was not amused when I laughed at that statement." This had been bothering Max ever since his conversation with the solicitor. He knew damn well that Henry never had any inclination to learn how the estate worked. Henry's father had also never been the outdoorsman and had relied heavily on his land steward's knowledge. The old earl had been much more interested in politics than sheep.

Several things, in fact, had been bothering him since that lengthy conversation. Mr. Knightsbridge had been irritatingly discreet while somehow still appearing solicitous. The only inclination of the man's opinions had been a disapproving frown when Mr. Knightsbridge had let him know that Lady Rivenhall was still living at the manor. And that Henry had left her a generous portion along with others. The man was not at liberty to disclose who those others were, only that the money had come from Henry's personal wealth and not from the estate's income. The why of Lady Rivenhall's continued residence at the hall was also not up for discussion. Max had been instructed to ask her himself. How did one bring up the topic? He certainly couldn't have his cousin's widow installed here at the estate without tongues wagging. He glanced across the table at Olivia.

"Mr. Knightsbridge is correct; my father is no longer in his position. Six years ago, when he became earl, Henry fired my father." Her lips twitched. "But you are misinformed. It is not Henry who has been taking care of the estate. I took over my father's duties. In fact, I have been handling things for quite some time."

Flabbergasted, Max leaned back in his seat. "Where are your parents now?"

Olivia's lips thinned, and sadness crept into her eyes. "My mother died shortly after you left. And my father...well, I'm not sure where he went when Henry let him go. And I don't care to know."

"Livvy." Max didn't know what to say. Her life had fallen apart, and he hadn't been here to help. He wished he could reach for her hand. But that was not who they were anymore. So, he just murmured, "Why didn't you write me?"

"I did," she said softly. Then she shook her head. "Doesn't matter. Henry took care of things when my life went upside down. But you are right, Henry much preferred town. He trusted me to run the estate. Speaking of the estate, I'm happy to give you a report on the status of things. And the offer for a tour is open whenever you are ready."

"Perhaps that can wait until Mr. Bromley arrives." Max reeled from her simple *I did.* She had written to him about her mother? No, he hadn't received any letters from her at all. Even though he'd written every week, like clockwork the first year he had been in Paris.

"Who?"

Max took a long sip of tea. "David Bromley, the land

steward I hired. He will be arriving later this week."

Olivia's chair scraped back as she abruptly stood. "You've hired a land steward?"

Her cheeks were stained red. Max stood as well, confused. "Yes, I'll need to have someone to oversee the estate. I haven't been groomed my whole life to take on this role. I'll need help."

"Maxwell Drake, of all the high-handed things. You should have consulted me first." She practically vibrated with emotion.

"Livvy, please sit down. Let's discuss this."

She shook her head. "Nobody knows this land better than I. If anyone should oversee the estate, it should be me."

"You?" His incredulity let his tongue loose before he could censor himself. "I mean, I have no doubt you are capable. But you must know that it is entirely improper on several levels. One, you are—"

"If you say woman." Olivia bit out in warning.

He held up his hands. "You are the widow of my cousin. It would be improper for you to live here still, especially since I am a bachelor with no family. And because you are the countess, it isn't right that you would labor at all, especially in a job as demanding as steward. Olivia, I know that Henry provided income for you. But if you need anything more. Please let me know."

Olivia's nostrils flared as she digested his words. "What am I to do with myself? Tell me, Max, because I cannot sit around some drawing room in London, gossiping and fending off lecherous lords."

"You are young and beautiful; you could find another husband easily." The words clawed at his chest as he said them out loud. But he needed to be fair to Olivia. He couldn't let his feelings mar her chances for happiness.

"Belhaven is my home." Her hands slapped down on the gleaming tabletop, rattling the china. "It always has been." Her bottom lip trembled—a small movement that mirrored the sadness in her eyes. Then she turned and raced from the room.

Max sat down heavily in his chair. That conversation had gone to shit quickly. How was he supposed to know she would be so upset about the bloody land steward? He ran a hand through his hair. And he hadn't even got a chance to give her the damn letter. Again.

Chapter Four

OLIVIA TOOK A large bite of honey cake. "I don't want to talk about it," she said around the mouthful of the sweet confection. *So delicious.* The creamy honey-flavored center of the cake melted in her mouth. Mrs. Buxley was a master at baking.

"Olivia, you are clearly overset. Please tell us what is going on," Charlotte asked. Her friend sat across the table from her at the tea shop. Her green eyes were bright with concern.

"I'm fine."

Susanna leaned forward, laying her forearms on the linen-covered table. "That is your second cake, dear."

"Is this about yesterday? We know that this time of year must be hard for you." Eleanor wrapped her arm around Olivia's shoulder and gave it a quick squeeze.

Olivia set down her fork. She glanced around the table at her friends. Susanna arched one auburn eyebrow in question. Ellie stared at her with serious eyes that missed nothing. And Charlotte sat with her hands folded atop her pregnant belly, patiently waiting for Olivia to disclose what was the matter. None of them would pressure her further, well, perhaps Susanna. But these caring women had supported her through the last year; if anyone understood, it would be them. She sighed. "It is about yesterday, but not in the way you think. He's here, at Belhaven."

"The new earl?" Susanna asked.

"Yes." She nodded. "He arrived yesterday, a day early. All alone, he came in like a specter out of the rain. And well, he's so…and he said…" Olivia didn't know where to start. Max had her emotions in such a tangle. Old feelings mixed with the new reality of the gorgeous man that now owned her home. The home where she could no longer live.

Olivia pinched the bridge of her nose. She knew that he was right. That her idea of staying on as the land steward was farfetched. Nobody on the estate would think it was strange; she had been filling her father's shoes for years now. But nobody outside of Belhaven Manor knew that she handled all the accounts, that she made the decisions about next year's planting and how many new sheep they needed to purchase. The guise that some man was handling the books was always there to protect her reputation. But damn it, she was the one who checked in on her families when she came to collect rents. She cared about her tenants. The idea that she would no longer be able to do that broke her heart.

"Tell us about Maxwell Drake. He is the missing cousin, yes?" Ellie asked.

"Yes, his father was Henry's father's younger brother. His father was a diplomat, and the family lived overseas often. Max used to come home with Henry during school breaks. He and Henry were fast friends."

Charlotte nodded. "I remember him somewhat. I think Lucius might have known him as well."

"We, the three of us, were friends." She ran her finger around and around the top of her teacup. "And then Max and I were more than friends." She glanced up and caught Susanna and Charlotte exchanging a look of wide-eyed surprise. "It was puppy love. We made sweet promises to each other. But then he left to take a job that his father arranged."

"What is his profession?" Ellie asked.

"He hunts down antiquities for a museum, I think. He is good with languages and figuring out puzzles. He said he has most recently been in Italy pursuing some painting. He always did like to unravel a mystery." Olivia smiled.

She remembered when Max had been obsessed with the stone outcropping on the eastern edge of Belhaven's land. The ancient stones called out to him, he'd said. She had enjoyed watching him walk around and take rubbings of the markings on the stones. His books open around him; he would compare the markings and try to figure out what language they could be. Max always muttered to himself when he was thinking, his long legs eating up the ground as he paced back forth with a book in hand.

"Italy! Fascinating," Susanna said. "When can we meet him?"

"Susanna, she hasn't even told us what he's done to upset her." Ellie frowned.

"This morning at breakfast, he reminded me that it

would be unseemly for me to stay on at Belhaven. That perhaps I should go to London and find a new husband. That he would help me if I needed anything." She scooped another forkful of cake into her mouth. "He's already hired a new land steward." She brandished her fork like a small sword, imagining she could stab Maxwell Drake in the heart.

"So, he plans to stay on at Belhaven?" Susanna asked.

Olivia shrugged. "I have no idea. I got so upset I didn't ask many questions. I just yelled at him and stormed out."

Charlotte's eyes widened. "That doesn't sound like you."

"He makes me so angry. I guess I harbor more resentment about the past than I thought. After a few months, his letters stopped coming. Busy with his new life, he forgot all about me." Olivia stabbed at the last piece of her cake. "Who will take care of my tenants now? Some stranger hired out of London?"

"He sounds dreadful. Domineering, careless." Ellie crossed her arms in front of her chest. "Good for you for yelling."

"Yes, dreadful," Susanna chimed in.

Charlotte laid a hand on hers. "I don't want to be disloyal. But he is right. You can't stay on at the Hall now that he has come to take possession. It will spark gossip. You can come to stay with Daniel and me while you decide what your plan for the near future will be."

"Thank you, but I have no intention of leaving him alone at Belhaven to make changes willy-nilly. He will need my guidance for there to be a smooth transition." Olivia propped her chin on her hand. "I will figure out something by the end of the year. I don't want to live in London. Henry understood that."

"Speaking of London. How is Mr. Galey?" Charlotte asked.

"Oh, fine. We've had a nice visit. He is so kind to check in on me."

Susanna batted her eyelashes dramatically. "He is very handsome and very kind."

Olivia chuckled. She knew that Susanna was already matchmaking. But what her friends did not know and never would, was that she and Mr. Galey would never be romantically involved. She would never again marry for convenience or safety. Henry had left her with enough money that she could live comfortably without a man. She was financially independent, now if she could only figure out what to do with the rest of her life.

"Not going to happen, Susanna. So just get the idea out of that pretty red head of yours."

Susanna frowned. "You are too young to live the rest of your life alone."

"And what about you? I don't see you choosing a husband," Olivia shot back.

"Ah, but I have not given up on the idea. I just haven't found the right man. I'm choosey."

All four of them laughed, including Susanna. As the daughter of the Earl of Dearborn, she was sought after for her dowry and connections. Tall, lithe, and with striking flame-colored hair, Susanna was beautiful. But what men never bothered to find out was that she was beautiful on the inside as well, kindhearted and whip-smart. Olivia agreed that she should be choosey. Luckily her father was indulgent and doted on his only child.

Mrs. Buxley appeared next to the table. Dark circles of exhaustion under her eyes gave Olivia pause. Typically the proprietress of the tea shop was bubbly and cheerful. "More tea, dears?"

Olivia nodded, and Mrs. Buxley poured hot water into the teapot. As she poured, she bungled the pitcher, and water spilled onto the table. "Oh, I'm so sorry! I didn't splash anyone, did I?"

"Mrs. Buxley, are you all right?" Olivia asked.

The older woman sighed and pushed back several errant strands of gray hair from her brow. "Truth be told, I'm not myself this week. Mr. Buxley had a small apoplexy."

"Oh no!" Olivia said. "When?"

"Last week. He's doing fine. The doctor said he was lucky, not too serious. But he has been having trouble with his right arm and hand feeling numb. The doctor's orders are for rest and no aggravation. Which means he has been stuck in bed and bothering me to death."

"Is there anything we can do to help?" Ellie asked.

"No, thank you. My daughter arrived yesterday to help me with the crusty old fool, so I can be here at the shop. I'll tell you because I know how much you all love the bookshop, but I think it's time for him to close it up and retire already." Mrs. Buxley glanced around and then lowered her voice. "It was mostly just a way to keep him out of my hair when he left the service."

"Close the bookshop?" Susanna gasped.

Charlotte and Ellie glared at Susanna. Then Charlotte smiled at the proprietress. "As much as we would miss the bookshop, his health is the most important thing."

Mrs. Buxley bit her bottom lip. "Now, I don't know if I can convince him to close it up, but certainly, he won't be able to run it for the next several weeks."

Olivia looked around the table at her friend's disappointed faces. And back up at Mrs. Buxley's harried expression. The poor woman, worrying about her husband's health and running the busy tea shop. The solution came to her in a flash. "I can help. Mrs. Buxley, will you let me run the bookshop while Mr. Buxley recovers? And if things go well, maybe in the new year, I could buy it from him. Perhaps he would feel better about letting it go knowing it would be in good hands."

Mrs. Buxley's mouth fell open. "But Lady Rivenhall, could you run a shop?"

"Of course, I could." She ran the estate. How much work could one bookshop be?

"No, ma'am. I mean, would a lady of quality be allowed to work in the bookshop?"

"I am a widow and have no one to tell me what is allowed and not allowed anymore." Olivia smiled. "I am certain I could at least handle the shop until Mr. Buxley is feeling better."

Ellie leaned forward. "I can help you."

"Me too!" Susanna said.

"Well now, what a relief it will be for Mr. Buxley to know the shop is being cared for. He has a shipment of stationary coming in next week and has been fretting about it. I'll be right back." She bustled off, disappearing through a door to the back of the shop.

Charlotte caught Olivia's gaze. "Are you sure this is what you want?"

Olivia nodded. "Don't you see, this is precisely what I need to keep my mind off the estate and Maxwell Drake. It could be just the thing to help me figure out what my next step will be. Plus, we can't let the only bookshop for miles and miles just close. It is really for the community."

"And our book club!" Ellie chimed in. "I'm happy to help. Lucius is busy with the new brewery. I'm at loose ends now that I have the house set up."

Charlotte smiled. "I will help as well." She patted her belly. "As long as there is a comfy chair for me to manage you all from."

They all turned to Susanna.

"You won't be able to keep me away. Mother and Father won't approve, but when has that ever stopped me before?" She shrugged. "I'll just pretend I'm shopping."

Mrs. Buxley returned to the table. "Here is the key to the shop. And thank you again. If you have any questions, you can go have a visit with Mr. Buxley. I'm sure he would talk your ear off."

Olivia accepted the iron key. The weight of it felt right in her hand, a sign that this was the right choice. This was the first time in a long while she felt a sense of purpose. Getting through the holiday without Henry had seemed impossible. And now, with the arrival of his heir, she was also forced to think about where she would live and what path her life should take. Olivia gripped tight onto the key. She would lose herself in running the bookshop. Perhaps if she kept busy, the answers to what to do with her life would come to her.

Chapter Five

TEA WITH HER friends was precisely what Olivia had needed to lift her spirits. She snapped the reins to gently urge her stubborn mares to keep going. The pair were new and needed a firm reminder of their job. "Come on, girls, it's freezing. Let's get home. How are you doing, Jimmy?" she called back to her tiger.

"Just fine, ma'am."

But moments later, it began to snow. The delicate small flakes drifting down grew into big fat snowflakes. Jimmy released the ribbons that tied back the hood of the curricle and lifted it in place. She was glad for the cover as her velvet bonnet did not have a wide brim, and snowflakes kept landing on her eyelashes. Once shielded by the cover, Olivia could enjoy the snowfall. The flurry of snowflakes fell steadily but melted on contact with the ground. Snow this early in December may be a warning of a cold winter this year.

They turned onto the estate's long drive. Olivia immediately felt on edge again. This place she had for so long called her home was not hers any longer. Maybe she should travel abroad. She used to have aspirations to see different parts of the world. Max and she had shared those aspirations, laying in the tall summer grass in their favorite spot by the stream they had talked of the Italian countryside, the clear blue waters of the Caribbean, the Great Pyramids of Giza. Olivia frowned. All those dreams had been replaced by the reality of her mother's illness and her father's cruel plans for her. It wasn't that Henry wouldn't have taken her abroad, but rather that she had felt so beholden to him for his kindness. She never wanted to ask too much, be too demanding. Belhaven Hall had become her safe place. It had been enough.

Max had gone on to travel the world. He had probably seen all those places they had spoken about. Men always had the advantage to do as they pleased. She tightened her cold hands on the reins. Well, she could do what she wanted now. She had no father nor husband to tell her what to do. The question remained: what did she want?

They turned onto the drive that led to the Hall. The bare branches of the trees sported a delicate layer of snow, like a table decorated with fine lace doilies. The house loomed ahead, and in front stood Maxwell Drake, his face tilted up to the sky. His arms stretched out to the sides, palms up. As they got closer, she could see that his eyes were closed and his eyelashes dusted with snowflakes. What was the foolish man doing?

As with each time she saw him, her stomach fluttered in response. She couldn't help but peruse his profile, the slope of his nose, his full lips, and his sharp jawline. She wanted to run her fingers across his cheek and lose herself in those amber eyes. She wanted to feel again the pull of attraction that had always been between them and see his lips curve into that half smile right before he kissed her. Olivia sighed at her inability to keep her thoughts in check. No use living in the past. He was the new earl, and she was a problem he needed to have settled.

She guided the curricle around the circular drive and pulled to a stop near Max. He didn't wear a hat, and his hair was dusted with snow. "What are you doing out in this weather?" she called out.

Max swiveled to face her. A grin stretched across his face. "It's been ages since I've seen snow. I looked out the window of the library and felt as giddy as a schoolboy when I saw the snowflakes." He walked over and held out a hand to help her down.

She couldn't help but return his smile. His enthusiasm for something generally viewed as an inconvenience was adorable. "Mr. Feeney, one of my tenants, swears we're in for a snowy winter. Says the signs are all there, something about woolly caterpillars." She shrugged. "He is rarely wrong."

Max didn't let go of her hand but gave it a tug instead. "Let's go for a walk."

"In the snow? I'm already frozen from the drive home from town. I'd prefer a hot cup of tea."

Max took hold of her other hand, and his eyes roamed over her. "Yes, I can see your nose is quite red. We'll go inside, but first, you must taste the snow. The first snowfall always tastes the best."

Olivia rolled her eyes and tried to tug her hands from his. "What nonsense. Snow doesn't taste like anything at all."

Max tipped his head back, and her breath caught as his tongue darted out to catch a snowflake. When he looked back down at her, his eyes twinkled with mischief. "Hmmm, tastes like Christmas."

Olivia laughter bubbled up in her chest. She tried to frown at his foolishness, but it was no use; the laugh escaped between her lips. Max laughed too; his deep chuckle filled the freezing afternoon air. *It tastes like Christmas.* What nonsense. She stepped back and turned to make her way up the stairs to the front door. She refused to be charmed once again by Maxwell Drake.

Chapter Six

MAX HUMMED 'GOOD Tidings to All' as he followed Olivia into the house. He'd been sitting at Henry's desk attempting to concentrate on the estate ledgers when he noticed the snowflakes swirling around out his window. Despite his aversion to the cold, there was something magical about snow. The fresh canvas it created as it covered the ground in a blanket of sparkling white. Perhaps the snow was a good sign.

Mr. Daniels appeared with a small brush. "Sir, let me dust off the snow." The man tutted as he circled Max attacking his jacket with a brush. Max should have called for his greatcoat, but in his enthusiasm, he had strode outside without thinking of bundling up.

Max watched Olivia hand her cape and bonnet to one of the footmen. She patted her hair and pushed a couple of loose pins back into place. Her smile had disappeared, and her polite façade was back in place. But he had made her laugh. And it had felt marvelous to crack her shell, if only for a moment.

She turned to the butler. "Mr. Daniels, I would love a pot of hot tea in the drawing room, please. I am frozen through."

"Yes, my lady. Right away." Mr. Daniels snapped his fingers, and he and the footman rushed away.

Max held out his arm. He didn't miss Olivia's hesitation before she rested her hand on his sleeve. "Here, let's get you by the fire." He led them to the drawing room, where a fire roared in the grate. A pair of stuffed chairs covered in a green paisley print sat in front of the fireplace with a wood table in between. Max stretched his legs toward the heat to warm his frozen toes. Across from him, Olivia sat stiffly with her hands neatly folded in her lap and her feet crossed at the ankles. He sighed.

"Olivia, I am sorry about this morning. It was not my intention to make you upset."

Olivia's gaze snapped up to his. "I know. I'm sorry I lost my temper. May I ask, what are your plans now that you have inherited?"

Max leaned back in his chair. "Honestly, I don't know. I don't think I am cut out to be a London lord. Politics and society and all that. I guess I will have to figure it out eventually."

"Do you still work at the Louvre?"

"No, a few years ago, I began tracking down items of value for private clients," Max hedged. He would never tell her that they were often stolen items he fenced for a tidy profit. That was the old him. "The last one, a painting, was an original Vasari that had been missing for decades. It took me months of research to find it." And minutes to lose it. He swallowed hard, remembering the night he almost died.

One side of Olivia's mouth quirked up. "You are the same as always then, single-minded when in pursuit."

He shrugged. There was something nice about being understood. He moved around far too much for any of his acquaintances to know him well. Since childhood, he learned to make friends easily and keep those relationships shallow so it would not hurt when it was time to move on to the next place. But Henry and Livvy knew him intimately. Their friendships had always been deeper.

A knock at the door signaled the arrival of the tea tray. A footman rolled a cart into the room. Max waited until the service was set and the tea poured before asking, "What was your business today in Marbury?"

"I was visiting with my book club," Olivia responded.

He lifted an eyebrow.

"My closest friends and I have a sort of book-lending club. We share the best books we have read each month. Mostly it is an excuse to get together and not to let busy lives keep us apart." She took a sip of tea and relaxed back against her chair.

"That's nice."

"Today, we found out that the owner of the bookshop in town suffered some ill health. Mr. Buxley is elderly, quite grumpy, and taciturn. His wife feels that he should close the shop; that it is too taxing for his health. She runs the tea shop next door, which is the true source of income for the couple along with his military pension." Olivia took another sip of her tea then glanced up at him over the rim. "I told her I would run the bookshop until the end of the year. It would be a shame for the only bookshop in town to close."

"That sounds like fun. What sort of books does he sell?" Max asked.

Olivia's eyes widened. "You're not going to say it's improper? That as the countess, I shouldn't be working?"

"That didn't work out very well for me this morning." He winked. "I'm a quick learner."

A small smile flitted across her lips. "The bookshop sells every type of book. There is no rhyme or reason to the shelves. Mr. Buxley simply puts new books in where ever there is room."

Max leaned forward. "That sounds horrible. How can you find anything?"

"It's a bit like hunting for treasure. You browse the shelves and choose whatever fits your fancy."

"You can't possibly think that is any way to shelve books."

Olivia scowled. "Well, I think it's delightful."

Then her lips twitched, and she burst into laughter. Her shoulders shook with it, and her eyes crinkled charmingly at the corners. "I'm just teasing. I can't wait to get in there and organize the place."

Max chuckled. "I'm glad to see you have not lost your mind. You must take me to see this place. I can help. In fact, I may not be able to sleep thinking about the disorganization."

botanist and is forever tinkering with my plants." Olivia exited the room with a swish of skirts.

Olivia's lover had been Henry's good friend? Perhaps he was mistaken about their relationship? But the man was staying here at the house with Olivia, having intimate conversations with her by the fire. They must be lovers. How long had Henry's *good friend* waited until he moved in on Henry's widow? Well, he would go find this Julien Galey, give him his letter, and size up what sort of man he was.

Max strode out of the room and down the hall past the dining room and to the stairs that led down to the ground floor. He made a left and headed for the back of the house. Spotting Mr. Daniels exit from a room down the corridor, he hurried to catch up to the man. "Mr. Daniels, would you know where Mr. Galey is? Lady Rivenhall said he might be in the greenhouse."

"No, sir. I saw him enter the morning room just a few moments ago. Shall I show you the way?"

"No, thank you. I remember." Max turned on his heel and headed back to the front of the house. He cracked open the morning room door silently, hoping to have an opportunity to observe the man for a few minutes before making his presence known.

"Are you warm enough, dear? Here let's get you covered back up."

The softly murmured words made Max step all the way inside. Covered back up? Who the devil was the man talking to?

Over by a large window, Mr. Galey stood in front of a potted plant with leaves as large as elephant ears. "Some water to wash the dust off. Yes, that's better." He gently wiped each leaf with a cloth. The man was so focused on his task he didn't even notice Max.

Max cleared his throat loudly, and Mr. Galey glanced up. "Oh, hello, Lord Rivenhall."

"Good afternoon, Mr. Galey. What is it you're doing? Do plants need to be dusted?"

"Around here, yes." Mr. Galey frowned at the leaves and gave another a swipe with his cloth. "The staff here water poorly and let dust build up. The leaves are where the plant soaks in light, which is essential for its growth. If there is a layer of dust on its leaves, it hinders this ability."

"Interesting. I did not know that." Max wandered into the room and glanced around. The walls were papered in a soft yellow giving the room a cozy feel. Olivia appeared to have a penchant for the sunny-yellow color. A large circular table graced the center of the room. There were six chairs set around the gleaming wood tabletop. At the farthest end of the room was a stone fireplace with a tufted settee in front. "Olivia mentioned that you were a botanist. Where do you work?"

"I was a professor of botany at Cambridge. I came to give a lecture to the Royal Botanic Society in London and met Henry quite by accident."

"Henry was in the Royal Botanic Society?"

Mr. Galey chuckled. "No. I literally bumped into him as

I was hurrying to the lecture. My papers spilled everywhere, and he was kind enough to help me gather them. Then he offered me a ride to the Society in his carriage. We became fast friends."

"That does sound like Henry. He would always be the first to help." Max laced his fingers behind his back. "You said used to work. Are you not still at Cambridge?"

"No, Henry bequeathed me some money in his will, and I have decided to fund a research trip to Brazil to study some of the fauna. I plan to write a text about flora and fauna in the Americas. It has been my dream."

Max raised his eyebrows. "When do you leave?"

"I'm still in the planning stage."

"Does Olivia know?"

Mr. Galey gave him a strange look. "Yes, of course. She has been a big supporter of my plans."

Surely, she would not be a big supporter of sending her lover halfway across the world. Max dismissed his thoughts. It was none of his business. He was here to give Mr. Galey the letter. "Mr. Galey, I have a letter that was left to you by Henry. It, along with one for Olivia, was given to me by the solicitor last week." He pulled it out from his jacket pocket.

Mr. Galey crossed to him to accept the letter. "Thank you," he said unsteadily. He immediately opened the letter to scan its contents. A grin spread across his face. When he looked up at Max his eyes shone with unshed tears. "Having something from Henry at this stage is like receiving an early Christmas gift. It's almost like hearing his voice again." Mr.

Galey's voice cracked, and he clutched the letter to his chest. "If you will excuse me." He brushed past Max, and hurried from the room.

Max swung around to stare out the door the man had just hurried through. What an odd duck. The man dusted plants, dreamed of writing textbooks, and seduced his friend's widow? He hardly seemed the rakish type. It was clear he had highly valued his friendship with Henry. That was a point in the man's favor. Max shrugged and turned back to exit the room. Perhaps he would find his way to the library. It was a perfect afternoon to spend reading a good book.

Chapter Seven

OLIVIA ENTERED HER sitting room and crossed to the divan that sat beneath the window. The snow outside still fell in gentle flurries that clung to blades of grass and fallen leaves. It probably wouldn't amount to much unless the snowfall became heavier. She curled up in the corner of the divan and pulled a blanket over her lap. Laying the letter open, she again ran a finger over her name. Henry's large loopy handwriting made her smile.

Dear Livvy, If you're reading this, then I've gone and made you a widow. I'm truly sorry for leaving you alone. Hopefully, I can come back as one of the ghosts and watch over you.

Olivia chuckled. "I wish you would come to visit me as a ghostly specter. Perhaps you could help me decide what to do next," she murmured. Then she continued to read.

I want to express how much I love you. You have been the best of friends. The kind of friend who laughed at all my stories, who kept my secrets, who always challenged me to know my value was not in how society viewed me but in who I was on the inside. You accepted the real me. I will forever be grateful.

Olivia ran a fingertip across the words. They had supported each other. His friendship had buoyed her through her mother's death and had saved her from a dismal future. When her father would have forced her to marry a man three times her age, a man who had been married as many times, Henry had swooped in and offered her an escape. Marry him, become his countess, protect his reputation, and in return, he would always keep her safe and cared for.

Henry had confessed to her that he had fallen in love with a brilliant young man named Julien. That they were careful to keep up the façade that they were just good friends. After all, Henry had had many friends. But since the death of his father, he had been under increasing pressure to marry. If Olivia consented to the marriage, it would help to protect his reputation and his secret relationship with Julien.

She and Henry never consummated their marriage but instead lived as happy companions. Henry spent most of his time in London, and that had suited them both. He always came to Marbury when she needed him for social events, and he had always come home for holidays.

Olivia sucked in a shaky breath. Henry had loved Christmastime. He would order the house decorated with greenery and bright red ribbon garlands. They entertained local friends at a huge Twelfth Night party. Henry had loved to give extravagant Christmas gifts. One year he'd given her five gold rings, mimicking the line from his favorite Christmas carol. Last year, after Henry's accident, no one had expected her to celebrate the holiday, and honestly, she didn't know if she cared to do anything this year either. Christmas frivolity had been Henry's strong suit. The holiday would never be the same without him.

I have always felt that because of our unusual marriage, you missed out on your opportunity to find true love. So, Livvy, my cautious English rose; this is my challenge to you. Do not waste away in widow's weeds mourning for me. I want you to travel, to take chances, and to fall in love. My relationship with Julien has made me indescribably happy, and you also deserve to find love, to find grand passion. But most of all, I wish for you to reach for whatever makes you happy.

Yours forever, Henry

Tears leaked out the corners of her eyes and rolled unheeded down her cheeks. Olivia wiped at them with the back of her hand. She had cried so many times over the loss of her friend. Henry had been her rock of safety in an uncertain world. He had given her a way to stay in the only home she had ever known. Their marriage had lifted her from a simple miss to the Countess of Rivenhall. But his words of encouragement hit home. Without Henry to hold her hand, could she take chances and explore the world outside of Belhaven and her beloved Marbury?

Love coupled with grand passion? She wasn't sure these things existed. Her thoughts swung to Max. Once upon a time, his kisses had inflamed her, and her adolescent heart had tumbled into his hands. But perhaps passion was transitory because when Max's father had called him to Paris for a job arranged with the Musée de Louvre, Max's letters, so regular at first, had just stopped arriving. The hurt and desperation she'd felt still stung even after all these years.

Pulling her thoughts back to the present, Olivia took in a deep calming breath. Henry's wish from the beyond was that she not waste her life in mourning. That she find grand passion. Now that she was a widow, dare she consider finding herself a lover? She no longer had anyone to tell her what to do, how to live. She was in control of her next move.

Olivia rose and crossed to pull the bell for her maid. The first step was to stop living in limbo. Ten minutes later, Franny poked her head through the door. "You rang, my lady?"

"Yes, Franny, I'd like you to get my trunks from storage. Tomorrow I would like to wear something other than black. It's time."

Franny's head bobbed up and down enthusiastically. "Yes, ma'am. I will tell Mrs. Peabody straight away."

Olivia walked over to the looking glass. "All right, Henry, here is the first step. Widow's weeds will be put away." She frowned at the woman with the pale face and the red-rimmed eyes in the mirror. "What's next? If you are haunting the Hall, please send me a sign."

Chapter Eight

"THANK YOU FOR meeting with me, Mr. Buxley."

"Thank you, Lady Rivenhall, for offering to take care of the shop. I just don't want to have to close the place up." He banged a fist against his chest. "This old heart of mine is not complying with my wishes, though."

Olivia passed the older man a cup of tea. He looked smaller somehow, wrapped in blankets as he sat in a worn wingback chair by the fire. His hair stuck out in tufts of white along the edges of his balding crown. She picked up her own tea and leaned back in her chair opposite him. "The bookshop is my very favorite place in Marbury. I know my friends would agree. I am happy to help keep it open."

"Ach, you and your friends are good girls. You always were my best customers." He gave her a watery smile. "My wife wishes for me to close it up. She says that I should spend my time more leisurely in my old age." He sighed. "Mayhap, I will think about it. Business has been dismal, and I don't think I can keep the place afloat anymore. My wife works hard at the tea shop, and it's enough, along with my pension, for us to live."

"Mr. Buxley, I know I can help bring the business

around. I may be a woman, but I have been running Belhaven for years and have made many changes that have produced new revenue. The bookshop is important. We need to have a place for books in the community."

Mr. Buxley huffed. "I have no doubt you could. Remember, I'm married to a woman who runs a successful business. I gifted her that building as a wedding gift. She created the tea shop from the ground up. You should have seen her back then, so much enthusiasm for her dream, for life. I never knew what she saw in an old goat like me, but I'm eternally grateful she married me, which is why I am seriously considering her advice to take it easy. But I'm not opposed to you comin' up with some ideas for the bookshop."

Olivia was taken aback by the sweet devotion the grouchy bookshop owner showed for his wife. She always thought that Mr. Buxley didn't like anyone. Olivia nodded briskly and blinked away tears forming in the corners of her eyes. She hadn't lied about the importance of the bookshop to her or to Marbury. She would turn things around. And if Mr. Buxley decided to sell it, she would make an offer to buy it.

This kernel of an idea had been growing since she read Henry's letter. Take risks, go after what you want. Of course, the advice was easier said than done. Her mother always told her to make sure to take care of others' needs, always taught her to swallow her own desires, to not ask for too much, to face life's disappointments with grace. But the bookshop would be purely for her own pleasure, a challenge to keep her moving forward now that she would have to leave the care of Belhaven to someone new.

She sent Mr. Buxley a smile. "Tell me, what orders are you expecting? Where do you keep your revenue books? Is there anything I need to know before I go to open the shop?"

"Well, the lock on the front door is a tad tricky. If you jiggle the key, it'll turn for you." Mr. Buxley began to explain the quirks of his place.

Olivia listened attentively. A ball of excitement formed in her belly. She was going to run a bookshop! She couldn't wait to spend her days organizing and planning and maybe even have time for some reading. This was going to be fun.

Chapter Nine

MAX BLEW OUT a long white stream into the cold air as he walked across the lawns at the back of the house. He headed through the orchard, walking underneath the bare branches that, in summer, would create shady paths and perfect spots to read a book. He and Henry would often come upon Olivia sitting on a low branch, her back against the trunk reading one of the many books she had pilfered from Belhaven's library.

He had loved to tease her about becoming a bluestocking and she would throw apples at his head. The truth was he and Henry were always jockeying to impress her. They would show off whoever had caught the biggest trout or climb into the high branches to pluck the ripest apples to give to her.

The sound of gurgling water got louder as he approached the stream. It cut through the eastside of the property. The waist-high grasses that grew along the bank were tan and brittle. A layer of frost covered their feathered ends and he brushed his hand over them as he walked past. He moved instinctively toward the bend in the stream. Their tree still stood tall, its gnarled branches stretching out over the water.

"Tell me what you read about Italy," Olivia had demanded that long-ago day. She'd rolled over onto her side and propped her head up with one hand.

"Well, the pope has his own tiny city right in the middle of Rome. He rules over it like a king."

She'd plucked a tall piece of grass and used it to tickle him behind one ear. "Phooey, I don't give a hoot about the pope. Did the book say anything about the ruins of the Colosseum? Or the canals in Venice? Did it describe the color of the Mediterranean Sea?"

He glanced over at her. "No, yes, and no. His description of Venice was quite nice. They get around the city on boats. And he talked quite a bit about its heyday during the Renaissance. But it was really more history than a travel log." He'd set his fishing pole aside and lay back into the soft grass next to her. The dappled sunlight through the tree above them made a streak across her nose and cheek. He leaned in and brushed a kiss to the freckles there. "We will just have to see for ourselves one day."

She had smiled up at him. "Promise?"

Max kicked a stone and it skidded across some ice and landed with a plop in the middle of the stream. He had broken that promise. He turned from the gurgling water and continued to walk. Seeing Olivia again had him turned inside out. He needed to exorcise the ghosts of who they used to be from his thoughts.

A while later he crossed back toward the house. The early morning walk had frozen his toes but rejuvenated his spirit.

Mr. Bromley should arrive on the noon coach, and Max planned to meet him and get him settled at the local inn for now. Once Olivia had a chance to meet and assess Mr. Bromley's qualifications, they could settle him into the house set aside for the land steward.

The house was the one Olivia grew up in, and with her father gone, Max had no idea what state it was in or whether it was ready to be occupied. However, he wouldn't make the mistake again of arranging the estate's future without discussing plans with Olivia first. He didn't want to upset her like he had the other morning.

He paused as he reached the front drive and stared up at the stone façade of the Hall. In fact, all he wanted was to keep her happy. He sucked in a deep breath of frigid air. Being near her again made him realize that his feelings for her hadn't faded. Even though he had buried them deep, all it had taken was one smile, one touch of her hand to unearth the love he'd always felt for her.

There had not been another woman who had come close to touching his heart in the last eight years. He kept his lovers at arm's length. Easy to do when one had to move on to the next job, the next country. Now he realized it had been easy to keep those relationships shallow because his heart had always been here, with Olivia.

The question was, what was he going to do about it? They were no longer the same two young lovers, wide-eyed and eager for each other. She had chosen Henry over him, and that scar still ached. She was his cousin's widow, which made his feelings all the more complicated. He had new responsibilities to care for and a new role that didn't quite fit yet. How did one go about being the Earl of Rivenhall? All he knew how to do was dig around in dusty libraries and back-alley markets.

He bounded up the wide stone stairs and pushed the door open himself. The footman hurried forward to take his coat, hat, and gloves. "Thank you, Stuart, is it?"

Stuart nodded his head. "Yes, sir."

"Good morning, Lord Rivenhall." The soft lilt of Livvy's voice rang out.

Max turned. Olivia walked down the stairs toward him; blue muslin skirts swirled around her ankles. After seeing her only in black for the past few days, the color was a shock. A darker blue velvet bodice snugly encased her ample bosom and ran down the length of her arms ending in white lace cuffs. His eyes roamed down her lush figure to the velvet-edged ruffles that adorned the bottom of the skirt. Realizing he was gawking like a randy schoolboy, he quickly moved his gaze to her face. The blue color complemented her dark brown eyes and gave her cheeks a rosy glow.

"You look as fresh as a summer day."

Her hand lifted, and she ran a finger over the lace trim of the neckline, and his eyes followed its path along the soft swells of her breasts. Lord, he wished he could sweep her up into his arms and bury his lips between those alluring, silken mounds. He swallowed back the impulse. He was most certainly going to hell for having such lustful thoughts about his cousin's wife.

"Thank you," she murmured. "I decided it was time to end the official mourning period. It has been one year and three days." Her gaze flicked up to the landing above as if she might like to bolt upstairs and change back into black.

He held out a hand. "Will you join me for breakfast?"

Olivia nodded and descended the last few stairs. She lay her hand in his and then gasped. "Your hand is freezing."

"I've just come from walking outside. I've worked up an appetite." He led her to the breakfast room.

"Did you wear your coat and gloves this time?" Her mouth quirked up at the corner.

"Yes, I swear I did. I am grateful to my grandmother for insisting that I outfit myself with a winter wardrobe before leaving Paris."

He held out a chair for her, and as she slid in he caught a whiff of her scent. It held a light tang of something that reminded him of fresh-baked biscuits. He stepped back quickly and moved around the table to his seat.

"How is your family? You said they have been in Paris?" she asked.

"Yes, for the past four years since my father passed away. My mother always liked Parisian society. She and my grandmother were not happy that I stayed with them for only two weeks." He grimaced. "I hadn't been home in two years previous to that. I feel a bit guilty for having such a short visit, but when I realized that it had already been so long since Henry died, I felt that I must make all possible haste to England."

Olivia nodded. "How long was the journey from Italy?"

"Two months." He didn't mention that it had taken him an entire month to recover from the attack. The scar left behind from the knife to his side still caused him pain if he twisted his torso to the left too quickly.

"I did not realize how far away Venice is."

"It is roughly a thousand miles from Paris. And the journey was delayed by bad weather in the Mediterranean." A footman attempted to pour him tea, but he held up a hand. "I'd prefer coffee if you have it."

"Certainly, my lord." The man hurried out of the room.

Olivia wrinkled her nose. "Coffee? I suppose that's a product of your travels. It smells heavenly but tastes terrible."

Max couldn't help but grin at her sour expression. "The coffee in Italy is made in the Turkish style, boiled with spices and sugar in a heated pot. It's rich and full of flavor. I used to drink several cups a day."

She frowned and took a sip of her tea. "I must admit I am jealous. You have seen all the places we once dreamed about together."

This was her first reference to their past relationship. He didn't know what the proper response should be. He longed to ask her about why she had given up on them. But his instincts told him it was too soon, so he went with, "Didn't Henry ever take you abroad?"

She shook her head. Her eyes focused on the teacup. Then her gaze lifted, and she opened her mouth to say something. "Max, why—"

"Good morning, everyone." Julien Galey swept into the breakfast room. He stopped in his tracks when he saw Olivia. "Darling, you look lovely." He moved to her and grasped both her hands. "No more black, ma chérie?"

Olivia looked up and shook her head.

"Is this because of the letter?" Mr. Galey asked.

Olivia nodded. "It's time."

Galey lifted one of her hands and kissed it. Max's instinct was to growl at the man, but he settled for a frown. Mr. Galey had impressively poor timing. Dammit, what had Livvy wanted to ask him?

"I feel the same." Galey moved around and took a seat. "In fact, I have decided to move forward with my trip."

Olivia's eyes widened. "You have?"

Would she be upset? Max watched her carefully for signs of distress but instead, a smile spread across her face.

"That's wonderful, Julien!"

Mr. Galey's head bobbed up and down. "As you said, it's time. I know that he would want me to follow my dream."

The two shared a long look. But not one of longing or even regret but more of shared understanding. Perhaps he had misjudged their relationship. The footman returned with a silver coffeepot. Max nodded, and coffee poured into his cup in a swirl of fragrant liquid. The footman retreated. Max added a splash of cream and took a sip.

Mr. Galey held his cup up, and the footman also poured him coffee. "How do you find it, my lord?" he asked.

"Delicious."

"Henry always kept good coffee beans on hand for when I visited. I cannot drink the swill you call tea."

Max chuckled. He glanced over at Olivia. "And how do you feel about such strong statements?"

She shrugged. "I am well aware of Julien's opinions. And he knows my distaste for coffee. As long as I'm not forced to drink it, I don't mind it at the table." She turned back to Mr. Galey. "When do you plan to leave for South America?"

"I hope for early spring. First, I need to arrange for passage, and thanks to Henry's generosity, I am able to hire what I need. It has only been my fear that has kept me home. But Henry is right; I need to pursue my dream. Life is too short to be afraid."

"I wish you luck in organizing your journey. Will you go back to town then?" Olivia said.

"I hoped you might have me still for Christmas." Galey once again took hold of Olivia's hand.

Why was he always touching her? Max took a sip of hot coffee to hide his frown.

"Yes, of course." Olivia's smile disappeared and her expression shuttered. She stood abruptly. "If you will excuse me, I must get going."

Max stood. "Where are you headed this morning?"

"I am going to go open the bookstore. I know Mr. Buxley usually opened it by nine."

"Can I ride with you? I planned to meet Mr. Bromley at noon. I could help you organize this morning."

Olivia bit her bottom lip. "Um, well, my friends planned to help…"

"Are they meeting you today?"

"Well, not today," she hedged.

"Livvy, it doesn't make sense for me to take a separate conveyance to town. Plus, this would be an opportunity for you to meet Mr. Bromley. I would value your opinion of the man."

"You would?"

"Yes, of course, I would. You have been running the estate, and even though I do still feel there needs to be a proper estate manager to handle the day-to-day, there is no one more qualified to assess Mr. Bromley's experience than you."

Olivia crossed her arms in front of her chest. "Humph!"

"Livvy, we both know that it would be improper for you to still live here and manage the estate. If anyone knew the extent of the work you have been doing, it would be a scandal. Please meet Mr. Bromley. He comes highly recommended."

Olivia sighed and blew out a long breath. Her eyes narrowed. "Be ready to leave in twenty minutes. And don't forget your coat." She left the room in a swirl of skirts.

Max sat down and scooped a mouthful of eggs. Blasted woman. Would he ever gain her trust back? "She didn't even eat anything," he muttered.

"She never does," Mr. Galey replied. "Only tea and sometimes toast in the mornings."

The fact that Mr. Galey knew intimate details about

Olivia's morning routine made Max scowl. It was none of his business about their relationship, he reminded himself. She was not his in any way. If only he could convince his heart of that simple truth.

Chapter Ten

OLIVIA GLANCED OVER to examine Max's profile as they walked up the street toward the bookshop. The cold air had reddened his cheeks, and his brown hair whipped about in the wind because, of course, he had forgotten his wool hat. The disarray of his appearance made him look young and so roguishly handsome. Her heart squeezed in her chest.

He tugged her closer with one strong arm around her waist. "Here stay close and let me block this biting wind."

Olivia frowned and stepped away. She did not want to be seen huddled next to a strange man on the street. Marbury was a small enough town that everyone knew everyone else's business. She reached into her pocket for the key to the shop.

"It's just there." She pointed. "Between the tea shop and the bakery."

Max nodded and stubbornly took hold of her elbow to guide her across the street. The only traffic was a couple of carts filled with wooden crates rumbling down the cobblestone street. High Street was one of three main streets through town that had long ago been paved. Because of this,

High Street was the main shopping thoroughfare, with the bakery, haberdashery, milliner, butcher, cobbler, tea shop, and bookshop.

They stopped in front of the shop. The cold breeze whipped fallen leaves in a frenzy around their feet. Max stomped his feet. "For goodness' sake. Let's get inside."

"Poor thing with your thin blood." She smirked at him and pulled out the large iron key.

"What is that?"

"The key to the shop, of course."

"It looks like a key to a sixteenth-century gaol."

Olivia ignored his comment and slid the key into the lock. It only made it halfway before sticking. She pulled it out, flipped it over, and tried again. It wouldn't go in all the way. Turning it back, she tried to keep it as straight as possible while inserting it into the lock. It made it in but would not turn in either direction. She blew out a frustrated breath.

"Here, let me try." Max made a grab for the key.

She elbowed him away. "No, I can figure it out. There must be some trick."

"Stubborn," Max muttered. "Just remember that I am freezing to death out here. You know, with my thin blood."

She gave the key a gentle jiggle and sent a small prayer to the heavens before turning the key to the left. It worked, and the key's scrape in the lock created a horrible high-pitched squeak that hurt her ears as it opened. "It sounds like it needs some grease. Here we go." She gave the dark blue door a shove, and they entered the tiny store.

Olivia shivered. "Would you mind starting a fire in the grate? Then we can light all the sconces and be able to see what we are doing."

Max nodded and got to work lighting a fire in the cast iron stove that graced the one corner of the front room. She couldn't help but notice the width of his shoulders as the material of his jacket stretched tight across them, nor did she turn away from the sight of his taut backside as he squatted down to strike the flint and light the tinder.

He certainly had put on muscle in the last eight years. Olivia bit down on her bottom lip. She wondered what it would feel like to run her hands across his broad back or be enveloped by those strong arms. Max rose, and she quickly turned away to assess the other end of the room. The last thing she needed was to be caught gawking at him. Max was far too charming; he did not need any encouragement.

The narrow store consisted of two rooms separated by an oversized opening trimmed in dark wood. All the wall space in both rooms was lined with dark wood bookshelves. In the front room, Mr. Buxley's mahogany desk sat near the large mullioned window that took up the entire front wall next to the door. The weak sunlight from the gray day outside did nothing to brighten the place.

Olivia walked to the desk and ran a fingertip through a layer of dust. "The shop has been closed for over a week now. We'll have to dust along with any organizing. Mr. Buxley said he was expecting a shipment of books this week.

How large, I have no idea."

First things first. She went behind the desk and spotted the small safe underneath. Delving back into her pocket, she pulled out the smaller key that Mr. Buxley had given her yesterday when she visited him. Unlike the front door, this lock turned smoothly. Inside was a smaller drawer with money separated neatly into piles of notes and coin by denomination. Clearly, Mr. Buxley's disorganization did not spill over into his money management. She closed the door before rising. Max already walked around with a long piece of kindling lighting sconces. Olivia hurried over to help, lifting the glass hurricane off the next sconce while Max lit the wick of the oil lamp.

They moved to the back room and lit four more. This room was more spacious and had a table with four chairs where patrons could sit down and read the newspaper. A pile of newsprint sat on the table under a layer of dust. In the back corner was a narrow spiral staircase that led up to a large hole in the ceiling. She gazed up at it, but the darkness above held no clues.

Max came to stand next to her. "What do you suppose is up there, attic space?"

"I have no idea, but I have often wondered. It doesn't have a hatch to close it off. It seems like an awful waste of heat." She glanced sideways at him. "Shall we take a look?"

Max grinned. "Absolutely."

He put his foot upon the first stair before she caught his arm. "Oh no, you don't. This is my store, at least for now. I get first peek."

"What if it's full of bats?" He arched one eyebrow.

"Then I will scream very loudly, and you may come to my rescue. Now kindly move out of my way."

Max chuckled but moved back. Olivia grabbed a handful of her skirts with one hand and the metal railing with the other. It was a bit cumbersome navigating the curved staircase. At the top, she looked down at Max. "Can you pass me a lamp, please?"

Max grabbed one of the oil lamps from the table and climbed up to hand it to her. "Livvy, be careful; this staircase is quite rickety."

She poked her head and shoulders through the opening, holding the lamp up high. "No bats," she called out. The space was quite a bit larger than she'd expected. Wood plank floors ran lengthwise across the space, as did the rafters above. A row of narrow windows looked out at the rooftop next door. The room was full of crates. *More books?* Olivia stepped up to the top step and swung her lamp around to the left. There were paintings of all sizes in gilt frames leaning along the back wall. A beautiful woman in a starchy Elizabethan collar stared back at her through the gloom. And right in the middle of the room was a large trunk, the kind one would take on a long voyage.

Olivia carefully backed down two stairs. She turned to look down at Max, who still stood on the second stair. "Well? What is at the top?" he asked.

"A lot of wooden crates, many paintings, and one rather

large trunk. Just storage, I guess. However, I cannot fathom how Mr. Buxley got any of it up these stairs. He is about seventy-five and thin as a rail." She passed him the lamp. "I'm coming down."

Max stepped off the stairs and set the lamp back in the center of the table. Olivia gathered her skirts again and slowly made her way down. It was impossible to see the next stair, and she had to carefully feel with her toe the location of each tread. Halfway down, she missed a step, and even with her grip on the railing, she lost her balance. Her stomach rose into her throat as she tumbled, but a pair of strong arms caught her, and she sucked in a deep breath of relief.

She looked up into worried amber eyes. "Thank you."

"Are you all right? Did you hurt yourself?" Max asked.

"No, thanks to you." She wiggled to get out of his embrace. But instead of setting her down, Max slid an arm under her legs to shift her higher against his chest.

"You just shaved a year off my life. I turned, and you tumbled right into my arms."

His forehead was wrinkled in concern, and his lips set in a thin line. Their faces were so close Olivia could see the dark brown flecks that made a starburst in the honey color of his eyes. Just a couple of inches closer and his lips could press against hers. She still remembered how his kisses had always made her feel hot and desperate low in her belly. Would it be the same between them? It had been so long since she had tasted true passion.

Max's gaze roamed down to stare at her mouth, and

Olivia's breath caught in her throat.

"Hello. Is the shop open? Olivia?" Charlotte and Daniel Weston strolled through the front room and abruptly stopped in the archway between the two rooms. Their shocked faces were comical.

Dear Lord. "Hello, you two. Um, this is Maxwell Drake, Henry's heir." She glanced up at Max. "These are my good friends, Lord Daniel Weston and Lady Charlotte."

Max stepped back from the staircase and set her on her feet. He looked between her and her friends. His cheeks flushed a charming red. "She lost her footing on the stairs…I caught her."

Chapter Eleven

DANIEL WESTON STEPPED forward. "Well, that's good luck. It's nice to meet you."

Max automatically shook his outstretched hand. He glanced at Olivia. She was straightening her skirts. When she looked up, she had a smile on her face. Likewise, the Westons both wore friendly grins. Relieved everyone planned just to ignore the fact he had been holding Olivia in his arms; Max returned their smile. "A pleasure to meet you both."

Next to him, Olivia stepped forward and embraced her heavily pregnant friend in a warm hug. "I didn't expect you to come help so soon."

"We were in town and saw the lamps were on as we walked past." Lady Weston's eyes sparkled with good humor. "This is so exciting. I feel like a small child sneaking into her parents' bedroom when they are gone."

Olivia nodded. "It does have a different feeling without Mr. Buxley being here."

"You mean a without his scowl watching your every movement through the store?" Lord Weston said archly.

"I told Mr. Drake…I mean Lord Rivenhall about Mr. Buxley's unique shelving system, and he insisted on helping with the reorganization."

"Just thinking about it made me itch," Max said. "And please, just Drake will do. It still feels strange to be called Lord Rivenhall."

Lord Weston nodded up at the opening in the ceiling. "I always wondered what was through there. What did you find?"

"Have a look for yourself," Olivia replied.

Max frowned. Damn it; he was curious to see for himself too. Weston grabbed up a lantern and made his way up the winding staircase. "Hmmm. I wonder how all this got up here? Mr. Buxley seems far too frail to heft anything up these stairs." His voice echoed from the attic space.

"That's exactly what I thought," Olivia called up.

When Weston came down, Max took the lantern and climbed to see for himself. Old treasures were his specialty. If anyone should assess what's in the attic, it should be him. When he lifted the light, his gaze immediately swung to the left, where a half dozen paintings leaned against the wall. Sixteenth-century by the look of the few he could see with the dim light from the windows and the small circle of light from the oil lamp. He moved the lamp around to look at the large trunk.

Curious, he climbed through the hole and scooted over to the trunk on his knees. He lifted the lid with a rusty squeak. The trunk was full of bottles of wine, stacked in neat rows. The green glass glinted as he raised the lamp and tried to read the labels. Barely legible, Max squinted to make out the words. Definitely French, and not wine but brandy. Well, well, French contraband. He turned and tried to lift the lid on a crate nearby. The lid was nailed shut. More and more interesting.

"Max?" Olivia's voice called up.

"Coming."

He backed out and descended the stairs. "Sorry, my curiosity got the best of me. The trunk is full of French brandy."

"Really?" Olivia exclaimed. The Weston's looked equally shocked.

"The small crates are nailed shut, but I doubt they are full of books. Between the paintings and the brandy, it seemed like your Mr. Buxley was using the attic as a place to store contraband goods during the war. It doesn't look like anybody's been up there in years based on the layers of dust over everything."

Olivia's eyes widened even further. "Crabby old Mr. Buxley trafficking contraband? I can hardly imagine it."

Max shrugged. "During the war, things were hard, and people turned to smuggling to make ends meet." It was how his father had gotten into the underground business of fencing artwork himself. The salary for a diplomat apparently had not been enough to fund his parents' extravagant lifestyle. His father had always resented how much harder he had to work than his titled older brother. Such was the luck of being a younger son.

Olivia tilted her head with a slight frown. "I suppose. It

is still hard to imagine."

Lady Weston clapped her hands together. "Well, where should we get started?"

Lord Weston took his wife's elbow and guided her to the table. "You should get started by sitting right here. You have been on your feet all morning."

"Pish! I feel fine. I can at least dust a bit."

Her husband crossed his arms and glared down at her. "You need to be off your feet," he said firmly.

Max fought back a smile at the stubborn look on Lady Weston's face. Luckily Olivia stepped between the couple. "Charlotte, we will start unloading the shelves, and you can be in charge of sorting the books into appropriate categories here at the table."

Lady Weston smiled. "Good plan."

They had only just begun to pull books off the shelves of one wall when the door opened again, and two ladies bustled inside along with the cold breeze. Both women were bundled in scarves and fur-lined capes, their hands hidden inside muffs. Max wondered if they were customers or more of Olivia's friends.

His answer came with Olivia's exclamation, "How did all of you guess I would be here today?"

The shorter of the two ladies unwound her scarf revealing a wide smile. "We were dropping off a pie for my father and Mr. Evans at the church. We saw you all through the window as we passed by."

The other lady pushed back the hood of her cloak to reveal jet-black hair and dark brown eyes set in an oval face. "Eleanor told me about Mr. Buxley's misfortune. I'm glad to hear you will keep the bookshop open."

Max raised his eyebrows at hearing her Italian accent.

"It's so nice to see you, Sophia. How was your trip to see your aunt in Cornwall?"

"Quite nice, thank you. Cold, but the scenery was magnificent." The woman gave a warm smile to Olivia. "How have you been? I see you have ended your mourning period."

Olivia ran her hands down over her blue skirts. "Yes, it was time. I received a letter from Henry which encouraged me to 'not waste away in widow's weeds.'"

"You received a letter from Henry?" Lady Weston asked. "How is that possible?"

Max stepped forward. "That's my fault. There were letters for Livvy and Mr. Galey in an envelope marked for the next Lord Rivenhall. The solicitor just gave them to me when I met with him a fortnight ago."

Olivia swiveled to face Max. She held out a hand. "Come, let me introduce you to my friends."

He came to stand next to her.

"These are the other members of my book club. Mrs. Eleanor Grisham." She gestured to the smaller woman. "She is the wife of Lady Weston's brother. And Mrs. Sophia Kingsley."

"A pleasure to meet you, Mrs. Grisham." He turned to Mrs. Kingsley. "*Piacere di conoscerti.*" He greeted her in Italian.

Mrs. Kingsley's eyebrows raised high. Then she tipped her head. "*Altrettanto.* How did you guess my native tongue?"

"Your accent gave you away." Max grinned. "I have just spent the last two years in Venice."

The friendly warmth in her eyes disappeared. She nodded stiffly. "And who are you?"

"This is Maxwell Drake, Henry's cousin. He is the new Lord Rivenhall," Olivia said.

Some of the tension in Mrs. Kingsley's shoulders relaxed. But her eyes still narrowed as she looked at him. Hmmm, he thought his friendly greeting in Italian would receive a warmer response. Mrs. Grisham also assessed him with a less than friendly gaze. "So, you are the missing heir waltzing into town a year after the funeral."

"Ellie," Olivia growled. "Behave, please. Today, Lord Rivenhall is lending a helping hand in organizing the store."

Max kept his smile in place. "Yes, Mrs. Grisham, I have just arrived in Marbury. It was a long journey from Italy. I did not receive news of Henry's death until September. I travel quite a bit in my line of work."

"And what is that, Lord Rivenhall?" Mrs. Grisham asked.

"Art and antiquities. I procure pieces for the wealthy elite."

Olivia arched an eyebrow. "You aren't working at the museum anymore?"

He shook his head. "Not for years. Art dealing is far more lucrative than curating collections at the Louvre."

"What are your plans now that you've inherited the title?" Lord Weston asked.

Max looked directly at Olivia and answered honestly. "I hope this will be a fresh start for me."

Olivia's eyes widened, but then she turned from his gaze. "Well, let's keep going. This place won't organize itself. We've been pulling books from that wall to start. Charlotte is assessing what categories we will need."

Debate about how to organize the shelves broke out around him. Max was glad not to be the center of attention any longer. He walked back to the shelf he had been emptying, his thoughts on Olivia. Having her in his arms again had felt absolutely right. He'd almost lost his wits and kissed her tempting full lips. That would have earned him a smart slap across the face, no doubt. *Don't be a fool,* he argued with himself as he plucked books from the shelf. You may still want her, but she barely tolerates you.

He turned to take his books over to the table. Olivia stood on her tiptoes to reach for the last book on a high shelf. Crossing quickly to help her, he easily grabbed the volume of poetry. She tipped her head to glance up at him in surprise, and he had the urge to kiss the tip of her pert nose. But he settled for a smile and handed her the book.

"Thank you," she said.

When they both stepped back, he turned right, and Olivia swiveled left. Her armful of books knocked into his stack, sending the books on top crashing to the floor. Several pieces of parchment skittered across the floor.

"Oops, sorry." He crouched to retrieve the books. Gathering the books and papers, he flipped one piece of paper over and realized it was a letter. He gathered two more before rising. "Look what fell from the pages of this book."

"Oh my, another letter," Olivia exclaimed.

"Three, actually." Max flipped them over to examine the long loopy scrawl. Interesting.

"More letters?"

"But we hadn't found any in months!"

"Let me see."

A chorus of female voices rang out in rapid succession. All four ladies gathered around him with wide eyes. "Another?" he asked.

"Yes. We've found a dozen love letters tucked in the pages of books, first here at the shop, and then Ellie and Lucius found more in a bookshop in London. They are all from the same shipment of books sold to the shop by a private owner. Mr. Buxley purchased part of that lot from the place in London. It has been an ongoing mystery to figure out who the couple is and what has become of them."

Mrs. Grisham nodded. "It seems their affair was a secret."

"She tucked the letters into books in her library to hide them. Maybe from her disapproving family," Lady Weston said.

"Or perhaps from her husband," Lord Weston chimed in, which earned him a disapproving frown from his wife. He just shrugged.

"Anyway, the address pages are torn off, leaving us with very few clues," Olivia said. "But we have enjoyed reading the letters. The author is quite effusive with his language."

Mrs. Kingsley winked. "And very naughty."

Max raised his eyebrows. "Well, that sounds interesting. You know you can use charcoal to find out the missing name and address."

"What do you mean?" Olivia asked.

"An imprint from the nub of the quill is left behind on the page underneath. You just have to rub lightly with charcoal to see it. Here, I can show you." He walked over to the desk and rummaged around in the top drawer for a piece of charcoal pencil. Then he returned to the desk where everyone had gathered. "I've done this often when trying to retrieve information from old documents where the ink had worn away."

He unfolded one of the letters, and indeed the address page had been carefully torn off. He flatted the first page of text then looked up at the group. "Should we read it first? The charcoal will make it hard after."

"Yes!" the ladies chorused.

Max was taken aback by their fervor. He picked it up and began to read aloud.

My love,

Seeing you with him last night has destroyed any joy I once felt in this life. I had to contain my jealous rage at observing his hand laying possessively at your waist. The smile you afforded him as the two of you danced almost overwhelmed me. I know you said you feel nothing for him, and you have avowed your affections for me in your letters. But not being able to hold you in my arms and be assured by the sweet kisses from your lips is torture. I must come to see you. Leave your window unlatched tonight. I will climb into your tower like a thief to steal any crumbs of affection you are willing to offer.

Yours always, J

"A bit dramatic, isn't it?" Max said. The letter was over the top in its sentiment, as though it was written for the theater. He glanced up and found everyone frowning at him.

"You have to have read the others," Olivia said. Then, she turned to her friends. "He had to have read all the others to understand."

The other ladies nodded, but Lord Weston smirked. "They are all like this. I will admit, the thread of the story does pull you in. The letters found so far are not in any order, so the ladies have been trying to decipher the whole picture."

That Max could understand, a mystery always appealed to him. "Shall we see if we can get a name or address off this?"

"Yes, please." Olivia stepped closer to peer down at the paper as Max began to lightly rub the charcoal pencil across the parchment in long even strokes covering the middle of the page. "Oh my," she breathed out softly as a name appeared.

"What does it say?" Mrs. Grisham asked.

"*Lady Diana Edwards, Number two Berkley Square,*" Max read aloud.

A collective gasp tore through the room. "Pardon?" Lord Weston exclaimed.

"Do you all know who this is?" Max asked.

Lady Weston nodded. "It's Daniel's aunt."

Lord Weston rounded the table to peer over his shoulder. "It can't be," he muttered.

Max worked carefully with the charcoal to move up the page and see if the return address would appear as well. It was harder to read, and he squinted at the parchment. "*Lady Althea Tangredi, 23 Exeter Street.* That doesn't make sense. Was her relationship with a woman?"

Olivia shook her head. "No, the other letters make it clear it was a man who wrote them." Her cheeks stained pink, and he wondered at the content of the other letters.

"Perhaps Lady Tangredi was his patron? It would make sense to use her name and address since the relationship was a secret," Mrs. Kingsley said.

"True," Mrs. Grisham said. "Oh my goodness, we have to go tell Susanna. She will never forgive us as it is for finding out something before she did."

Olivia nodded. "I can't leave the shop just yet. And we are meeting the new land steward at noon. So, I'll let you take the letters to show Susanna. I will visit later in the week and get my chance to read them."

"Are you sure? It doesn't seem fair," Mrs. Grisham said. "Why don't you keep them and we will all come by Belhaven tomorrow afternoon to read them together."

"We should head home. I would like to write my brother immediately," Lord Weston said to his wife.

Lady Weston nodded. Her husband helped her to her feet. "Olivia, you keep the letters, and we will see you tomorrow."

Olivia's friends bundled back into the capes and scarves and hurried out the door. Once everyone was gone, Max picked up one of the other letters, which sat still folded on the tabletop. He waggled his eyebrows at Olivia. "Shall we read some more?"

"No, we can't. I agreed we would read them all together tomorrow." She glanced at the letter in his hand, and Max grinned at the look of longing on her face. Olivia shook her head. Then she bit her bottom lip. "But they wouldn't have to know, would they?"

Chapter Twelve

THE COLD AIR slapped Olivia in the face as they exited the store shortly before noon. She felt a little guilty for reading the letters without her friends but having a partner in crime made her feel better. Max's mischievous grin had been irresistible when he asked her if they could read the letters. She glanced sideways at him as she locked the front door.

"At first, I thought the letters to be ridiculously over the top, but his sincerity won me over." Max whistled softly. "And that last one, if only I had words like that to seduce a woman."

She pursed her lips. The idea of Max sharing intimate words like those in the letter with any woman left a sour taste in her mouth. Not that it was any of her business. She turned and found Max waiting with his elbow winged out. She slid her hand through and laid it on his sleeve. He persisted in being charming, and it was starting to wear down her carefully built wall of self-preservation.

"The thing that bothers me is that the letters don't follow each other chronologically," Max said. "It's like an itch I can't scratch. I must know the entire story. Would it be possible for me to read the others? Does it all make sense as a whole?" His brow furrowed in consternation.

Olivia chuckled. "Yes, I can gather the others if you'd like to read them. You never could leave a good mystery alone."

Max shrugged, and his smile returned. She had a sense that he appreciated being understood. It made her wonder: Where had he traveled? What sort of art had he hunted? Who were his friends? Was he happy with the path he had chosen? Did he miss home? Had he missed her?

Olivia pushed away all her questions. They were not friends anymore, and his life was not her business. When she thought of his abandonment, the wound still throbbed. Spending Christmas without Henry would be hard enough; she did not need to dredge up her old feelings for Max. The best thing to do was focus on the bookshop and settle things at Belhaven as quickly as possible. Then she could decide what to do with her life in the new year. Olivia sighed. Whatever that might be.

Max tugged her closer. "Cold?"

She shook her head and tried to pull away. But Max stopped suddenly; his hand gripped hers. "Look at the festive display in that window."

Olivia followed his gaze. Mr. and Mrs. Ford had decorated the front window of the general store with greenery and bunches of holly berries. Three shelves displayed a myriad of items that would make nice Christmas gifts. A dusting of flour on each shelf made it look like they were covered in snow. And the center of the display featured a beautiful snow globe. A tiny painted couple skated in a winter wonderland beneath the glass dome.

Max pulled them over to stand in front of the window. "Look at that. Oooh, that pocket watch is tops, and look at those toy soldiers. I loved playing with toy soldiers as a child." His face lit with excitement. "What do you fancy?"

Olivia stared at the globe. She used to have one when she was a child. A gift from her parents at Christmas. That scene had been of carolers singing in front of a grand home. Her mother always loved to go caroling. She pointed to the ice skaters. "I quite like that one. I do enjoy ice-skating."

"Yes, I remember you would skate circles around Henry and me."

Henry and Max had been bloody awful skaters. But she loved gliding across the ice and the floaty feeling of gracefulness that the skates provided. Her mother would always have hot cider waiting as the three of them tumbled into her kitchen with red noses and rosy cheeks. The pond at the end of the lane by her house was the best place to skate.

Henry had been too scared to tell Mr. Daniels he was off skating. Before she died, his mother had always been afraid he would fall through the ice and rob his father of his heir. The whole household was careful to watch over a very annoyed Henry. So they always warmed up in her mother's kitchen, where Anne listened attentively to their escapades. Olivia's heart ached at the fond memories.

Max nodded his head toward the festive window display.

"You know it might be a good idea to decorate the window at the bookshop for Christmas. You could feature your favorite books and perhaps increase sales. This window is so cheerful."

Olivia shrugged. Window dressing was a waste of time. She did not plan to celebrate Christmas without Henry. He was the only one who made the holiday special. How could she possibly enjoy the season without her best friend? The corners of her eyes filled with tears. She tugged Max away from the window display.

They continued down the street. Two doors down, the dressmaker shop had their window display done up for Christmas as well. The centerpiece of the window was a beautiful dress of red silk. The design featured an off-the-shoulder style that would beautifully showcase a necklace. It had puffed sleeves in airy tulle and full skirts with a damask print in pale gold. Olivia caught her breath. The dress was exquisite.

Max paused and glanced over at her. She avoided meeting his gaze and instead stared at the window display. A pair of heeled gold slippers sat next to the dress, surrounded by a wreath of greenery. She sighed in feminine appreciation.

"We should head to the coaching inn to meet Mr. Bromley," Max said softly.

"Yes, of course," she replied. They walked down to the end of High Street, where it intersected with a large square of green space in the center of town. The grass was more brown than green, and the water in the fountain was frozen solid.

The bare branches of the trees arched over the square and crisscrossed the blue sky above. The wind seemed to increase its bluster as they crossed the frosty grass. "By the weekend, the festival will be set up here in the square. It runs for eight days. So there will be plenty of Christmas cheer for you to enjoy." Olivia hunched her shoulders against the wind.

Max abruptly pulled them to a stop. "But not for you to enjoy?" He turned to face her, blocking the wind with his broad back. "What's going on? I can't help but feel you are trying your best not to enjoy the Christmas season."

How did he know? "Don't be ridiculous," she replied. "We'll be late."

Max put a finger under her chin and tilted her head, forcing her to meet his gaze. "Livvy, what's going on?" he repeated.

His eyes soft with concern, he waited patiently for her to divulge her thoughts. He always had a terrible talent for seeing straight into her soul. A tear sneaked out and ran from the corner of her eye. She tried for a smile, but it wobbled, and she gave up trying to pretend. "Henry loved the Christmas season. We always spent December at Belhaven. We had friends over for dinner parties, and the house smelled of fresh greenery. He always came up with the most extravagant gifts." She rolled her eyes. "No matter how I protested that it was too much, he would try to top his gift from the previous year."

"Sounds just like his father. He always loved elaborate surprises."

"It's not that I'll miss the presents. It's that...well how can it be Christmas without Henry? I certainly have no talent for entertaining and creating fun. That was always Henry's strong suit." More tears rolled down her cheeks. "It feels wrong to celebrate when he is gone."

Max brushed his thumb across her cheek, gently wiping her tears away. Then he brought his palm up to cup her chin. His amber eyes glowed with understanding and something else far more tender. Olivia recognized that half smile of his one second before Max leaned in to press his lips against hers. The first brush of his mouth was brief as though he was testing his memory of her lips. The second press of his lips lingered longer. He changed the angle of the kiss, and they sank against each other.

His lips were soft and gentle as they nibbled and tasted hers. Olivia parted her lips on a sigh of pleasure. The feel of his mouth was so familiar, as though she had been kissing him every day for the past eight years. And the desire that coursed through her took her by surprise. It had been so long...she took hold of the lapels of his coat to keep herself steady.

Slowly, fractionally, Max pulled away.

Olivia opened her eyes. "Why did you do that?"

He brushed his thumb across her bottom lip. "I never could stand to see you cry."

She blinked and willed her brain to begin functioning again. She shouldn't be kissing Max in the public green. She shouldn't be kissing him at all. Or rather, he shouldn't be kissing her. Olivia took a large step back. "This is entirely inappropriate."

Max stared at her for a long moment. Olivia looked down and adjusted her scarf to escape his direct gaze.

"Livvy—"

"I think we should go and meet Mr. Bromley." She had no intention of talking about the kiss. "The stage should be arriving any minute."

"All right." Max held out his hand.

But she ignored it and began walking toward the inn. She couldn't touch him right now. He was like Christmas, sparkly and cheerful, but not for her. She would, of course, make gift baskets for her tenants and go to church on Christmas morning. But all the fanfare and trimmings were for other people—those who still had some Christmas spirit left. Hers had died on the side of the road last December.

Chapter Thirteen

MAX WAS IMPRESSED. He hid his smile behind his glass of ale as he watched Olivia. She had spent the last hour interrogating Mr. Bromley. To his credit, the man had answered every one of her questions respectfully, even though Max had already hired him for the position. Olivia slowly started to warm up to Mr. Bromley, and the two of them had been deep in discussion about crop rotation for the last quarter hour. Max sat back and enjoyed his excellent ale. He had nothing to offer the conversation, and frankly, the other two probably forgot he was sitting here.

It allowed him the opportunity to think about kissing Olivia. The kiss they shared had shaken him to his very soul. He hadn't meant to kiss her. He really hadn't. But what he said to her had been true; he couldn't stand to see her cry. He just meant to offer a small gesture of comfort, but the kiss had tumbled him back in time to the breathless, frantic kisses they used to share. That same desperate desire had thrummed in his veins as he tasted the sweetness of her mouth. Her soft sigh had enticed him to deepen the kiss.

Max took a long gulp of ale. Olivia had firmly put him in his place afterward. He knew he'd overstepped the boundaries that she carefully constructed around herself. He sighed. How did one go about winning back the love of your life when the woman in question loved someone else, mourned someone else?

"What do you think, Lord Rivenhall?" Olivia's voice penetrated his thoughts.

"Pardon? Sorry, I wasn't paying attention," he said.

She frowned. "We were discussing Mr. Bromley's living arrangements. I informed him that the house set aside for the steward would need to be cleaned out and most likely a few repairs done before it could be ready for him. Is it all right for you to pay for his room at the inn until the house can be readied?"

"Uh, yes, of course," Max replied. "Will that work for you, Mr. Bromley?"

David Bromley nodded. "Yes, that is fine. I am a bachelor, so there is no need to rush. I'll be just fine here. If the food is always as good as today, I will be eating like a king." He patted his stomach.

"Mrs. James's food is always good." Olivia smiled. "If you will both excuse me, I will just go say hello to a friend. Good day, Mr. Bromley."

Max and Mr. Bromley both rose and watched Olivia walk across the room toward the long bar. A handsome blond man smiled broadly at her as she approached. Max frowned as they clasped hands, and the man bussed her cheek.

He forced himself to move his focus back to Mr. Bromley. "So, we will see you Friday morning to have a tour of the estate?"

"Yes." Mr. Bromley lowered his voice. "I am relieved to have passed the test with Lady Rivenhall. She certainly knows what's what."

"She certainly does." Max shook Mr. Bromley's hand. "See you later this week."

Then he walked across the main room to where Olivia spoke with the blond man. She tilted back her head and laughed at something the man said. The sounds warmed his heart but also ignited a small flame of jealousy in his chest. He lengthened his stride. "Hello."

Olivia turned, a smile still played across her lips. "Drake, may I introduce you to Mr. Lucius Grisham. You met his wife this morning. He is Lady Weston's brother."

Ah. His jealousy faded. "It's nice to meet you, Mr. Grisham," he said with a nod.

"Nice to meet you as well. I have heard plenty about you already." Mr. Grisham grinned as he looked him over.

Olivia gave the man a sharp look. But it just made Mr. Grisham chuckle. "Well, if you will excuse me, I need to get back to my deliveries." He hefted a small barrel from the floor to rest it atop his right shoulder.

"Mr. Grisham makes the ale you drank. He has just opened a brewery right here in Marbury," Olivia said.

Max raised his eyebrows. "That was the best tasting ale I've had in some time."

"Thank you. That means a lot. Mr. James is my first big

customer. He serves three of my brews here in the dining room."

"Well, I'd like to order a barrel for Belhaven. Can that be arranged?"

"Certainly!" Mr. Grisham's face lit up. "Good day to you both. Must be off." He turned and left through a door in the rear.

When Max glanced down at Olivia, she contemplated him with soft eyes. He thought perhaps she was going to cry again. "What's the matter?" he asked.

She shook her head. "Nothing. That was very kind of you. To support his business, I mean. It will mean a lot to him and Eleanor. Thank you."

Max rubbed the back of his neck with one hand. "His beer is excellent. I wouldn't have ordered it if it wasn't."

The smile she aimed at him felt like the sun emerging from behind gray skies, and its warmth hit him right in the center of his chest. "Do you mind if we stop and pick up the post since we are in town?"

"Not at all," Max replied.

Olivia slid her arm through his as they stepped out of the inn, and the warm spot in his chest spread. "Just around the corner," Olivia said.

They walked next door to where the carriage house housed fresh horses and fixed broken wheels and such. At the corner of the building was a small receiving room where the mail was held after being dropped off by the mail coach. Olivia approached the middle-aged woman behind the counter. "Good afternoon, Mrs. Kirk. I would like to pick up the post for Belhaven, please."

"Good afternoon, Lady Rivenhall. Surely, just one moment." The lady bustled to the back of the room to pull a stack from a wooden cubby. When she returned, a wrinkle appeared between her eyebrows. She leaned across the counter with a frown. "There is a letter here for Lord Rivenhall, and I didn't know if it to be a mistake."

"No, Mrs. Kirk, it is not a mistake." Olivia gestured to him with one hand. "This is the new Lord Rivenhall, Maxwell Drake. He just arrived in town earlier this week."

The lady's eyes widened, and she gave a small curtsy. "Good day to you, Lord Rivenhall. I had not heard."

"Good day to you, Mrs. Kirk." Max tipped his hat. "I am surprised there is post for me already. I did not think anyone knew where I was."

Olivia accepted the small stack of mail and passed him a letter. The flowing script belonged to his mother, and when he saw the return address was London, he sighed. How had they made it to England so quickly? He'd left them in Paris only three weeks ago. His mother had been quite excited about his new status, and at the time, the calculating gleam in her eye had made him roll his eyes. But if they were in England, she must have plans to take advantage of his new title. He raised his gaze from the letter to find Olivia watching him thoughtfully. "It's from my mother," he explained.

"Ah." She nodded.

He broke the red wax seal and unfolded the pages. Scanning the missive, he let out another long sigh. Just what he needed.

"What is it? Bad news?"

Raising his gaze, he said, "Livvy, we better get home."

Chapter Fourteen

MAX HELD THE reins steady as he guided the horses to make the turn onto Belhaven land. It wasn't as though he didn't love his family, but having them unexpectedly arrive *en masse* would be its own trial. His grandmother, mother, and younger sisters could show up at any moment. The letter had been postmarked two days ago, and it was only a day's travel from London to Marbury. He'd hoped to have some time to get his feet under him with his new role before he invited his family to come visit. And with Olivia and Mr. Galey living at the house, it made the situation all the more complicated.

He glanced over at Olivia. She stared straight ahead with a furrowed brow. Then, as though she sensed his gaze, her eyes flicked to meet his. He gave her a tight smile. "They were excited to learn of my new position. I think my mother always wished the title for my father. Although she got along well enough with Lady Rivenhall, there was always a bit of jealousy on my mother's part."

"And your sisters, how old are they now?" Olivia asked.

"Genevieve is nineteen, and Louisa is fifteen." Max couldn't believe how his sisters had grown into young ladies.

In his mind, they would always be in pinafores, climbing into his lap and peppering him with questions about his travels. When his father died four years ago, he knew it had been hard for all the women in his family. His father had been an exuberant force of nature. He had approached everything in life with good humor. He was also a man that created his own opportunities and he had provided well for his family. Max regretted not being around more often the past few years, but the burden of supporting his family had fallen to him, and he'd had to hustle to keep paying the bills.

"I'll be happy to meet them all finally. In all the times you came to Belhaven, your family was always overseas." She nodded her head as though she was convincing herself. "We will tell Mrs. Peabody of their imminent arrival and get everything ready."

Up ahead, he could see two large carriages in the circular drive. He and Olivia exchanged a startled glance. "I hope you meant that because your opportunity is at hand. It looks like they beat us here."

Olivia grimaced. He pulled the curricle to a stop behind the second carriage. Climbing down, he held out a hand to help Olivia disembark before turning to the chaos in the drive. His mother was speaking heatedly to Mr. Daniels. Ginny was instructing two footmen to unload the trunks from the second carriage. Grand-mère Lucinda was just exiting the carriage with the help of another servant. Her wig and oversized hat bumped against the top of the door opening knocking the whole thing askew.

"Grand-mère, let me help." Ginny rushed over to help straighten it.

"Thank you, dear."

His other sister, Louisa, leaned against the carriage wheel not five feet away, her nose buried in a book. He strode closer. "Hello! What have we here, a traveling circus?"

Everyone paused and looked over at him. A chorus of "Max!" rang out. Louisa was the first to fling herself into his embrace. He wrapped one arm around the petite girl. Ginny was next. She kissed him on each cheek and then again on the first. "Brother, are you surprised? We've come to spend Christmas with you!"

"I am, as I only received Mother's letter today. I haven't even had time to warn the staff." He walked over to his grandmother and kissed her paper-thin cheeks. "Grand-mère, how was your trip?"

"Terrifying, English roads are the worst in all of Christendom." She laid a hand on his cheek. "I told Marguerite we would be intruding. But she is determined to see for herself what you have inherited."

Mr. Daniels spotted Olivia, and the relief on his face was comical. "Lady Rivenhall, I'm so glad you're here. You have unexpected guests."

"Yes, Mr. Daniels, this is Lord Rivenhall's family." Olivia turned to his mother with a warm smile. "Welcome to Belhaven Hall, Mrs. Drake."

"Thank you…Lady Rivenhall." His mother replied with an arched eyebrow.

Max hurried over. "Mother, it is lovely to see you. If somewhat unexpected." He bussed her cheeks.

"I wrote you," she said.

"Yes, we just received the letter today. In fact, about an hour ago. How did you travel here so fast?"

"Yes, well, you only stayed in Paris for such a short time. And the day you left, we all agreed how much we missed you already. So I decided we should return to England and visit you for Christmas!" She raised her hands and kissed him again. "We left just a few days after you."

Olivia spoke quietly to Mr. Daniels. "We will have them stay in the Rose, Violet, and Gardenia rooms. Have the fires started and the trunks unpacked. Tea in the blue drawing room."

Mr. Daniels bowed and hurried inside.

"Allow me to make proper introductions. Mother, this is Henry's wife, Olivia. Lady Rivenhall, my mother, Marguerite Drake." His grandmother and sister joined them. "My grandmother, Lucinda Stanley. My sisters, Genevieve and Louisa Drake."

"It's a pleasure to meet you all." Olivia nodded her head. "Now, I think we should all get in out of the cold." She gave Max a pointed look.

"Yes, of course. This way." Max offered his grandmother his arm. They all trooped inside. Capes and muffs were collected, and Olivia led the way into a drawing room he had not been in yet. The well-appointed room was decorated in soft blue and gold. A young maid was on her knees, stoking the fire into a blaze. She turned around as they entered, her eyes round as a startled doe. Max recognized her as the maid who had thought he was a ghost the first night he arrived. He sent her a friendly smile.

"Thank you, Enid. That will be all," Olivia said.

The girl popped up, made a short curtsy, and scurried out of the room. Olivia gestured to the seating area near the fire. "Please, come sit down where it's warm."

He helped his grandmother get settled on the settee. She patted the spot next to her. "Sit next to me dear. I didn't see enough of you in Paris."

His mother took a seat next to Ginny on another settee while Louisa wandered around the room, her book tucked under one arm. She wasn't one for polite conversation, so he was surprised when she was the first one to speak.

"This is a lovely room, Lady Rivenhall. The colors are soothing." Louisa picked up a small figurine from the mantel. "But this is quite ugly."

"Louisa!" his mother said. "Apologize at once."

Louisa's eyes widened. "I'm sorry. I should have kept my opinion to myself."

Olivia's lips twitched, and Max guessed she was holding back a laugh. "Thank you for the compliment about the room. Blue is my favorite color." She smiled at Louisa.

The conversation stalled. "So, Mother, you said you would be visiting through the Christmas holiday?"

"Yes. Won't it be nice to spend Christmas together as a family? It has been too long. I have decided we will spend the upcoming year in England. This spring will be the perfect opportunity to launch Ginny into society. Your new title affords her an opportunity to find an excellent match. I expect you to do whatever you can to see both your sisters settled properly."

"Of course, Mother. I'm happy to help in any way," Max replied. And it had begun. Not that he blamed his mother for her ambitions. Only that he hadn't even had time to think of himself as the Earl of Rivenhall, let alone think about socializing with the quality.

"And you should think about finding a wife this year, too. You will need to beget an heir."

Max opened and closed his mouth but had no reply to his mother's blunt words.

Ginny chuckled. "Now you know how I feel, dear brother."

"Perhaps, we can all have some tea before you begin handing out directives about your children's lives, Marguerite. There is plenty of time for all of that," Grand-mère said.

Right on cue, Mrs. Peabody arrived with the tea cart. She arranged the tea service on a low table and directed the maid to set down the sandwiches and biscuits next to it. The two women left, and Olivia poured steaming cups of tea for everyone. As his sisters piled food onto small plates, Max watched Olivia, mindful that she hadn't eaten anything for breakfast. She sipped on her tea but did not eat anything.

"This is delicious. I'm starved," Ginny said around a mouthful of biscuit. Their mother shot her a warning look, and Ginny swallowed her food before continuing. "Thank you. The food is lovely."

His mother shook her head. "I don't know what I will do with the two of you." Her gaze was soft as she looked at her daughters, though, and Max knew his mother was all bluster and no bite.

"We could have a dinner party to introduce you to local society. Get your feet wet, so to speak." Olivia's quiet suggestion surprised him.

"I think I could handle that. How many people are we talking about?" He filled a plate with two cucumber sandwiches and a lemon biscuit, all Olivia's favorites. He offered her the plate, and before she could protest, shoved it into her hands.

"Let's see; there are four or five families in the area that are part of the quality. I'm sure they will all know you are in town before the end of the day now that Mrs. Kirk knows you are at Belhaven. We could start with them." She nibbled delicately on a sandwich triangle, then as though finally realizing she was hungry, she consumed it in two bites.

"Lovely!" His mother clapped her hands together. "Christmas Eve is in one week. Let's do it then. I do love the Christmas holiday." She turned to Olivia. "Unless there is another party happening already?"

Olivia shook her head. "Not that I know of." She stuffed the lemon biscuit into her mouth.

Ginny scooted to the edge of her seat. "A Christmas Eve dinner party sounds wonderful. We can decorate and play games, and I can play the pianoforte and lead the singing of carols."

Olivia's skin paled and her eyes flicked back and forth between his sister and mother as they started planning the dinner party. Louisa rolled her eyes and snatched another sandwich from the tray before she plopped down next to Olivia. "You'll get used to them. They are forever planning parties. The only thing they love more than a party is a Christmas party."

Olivia rose to her feet. She clasped her hands tightly in front of her. "If you will all please excuse me, I will just go check with the housekeeper that your rooms are prepared." Then she turned on her heel and fled the room.

It was the only word to describe her mad dash toward the door. In less than a moment, she was gone. Max frowned. It must be all the talk about Christmas. Hadn't she just confided in him about her aversion to celebrating this year? Unfortunately, there would be no getting around celebrating Christmas with his family around. He would make it his mission to make Christmas as wonderful as possible for Olivia. After all, Henry would have wanted her to enjoy the season.

"Maxwell, what is Lady Rivenhall still doing here? Shouldn't she have vacated Belhaven by now?" his mother asked once the door had shut behind Olivia.

"It took almost a year for the solicitor to find me. She has been taking care of the estate. Plus, this is where she has always lived."

"What do you mean?"

Max took a sip of tea and debated how much to tell his mother. "Olivia's father was the land steward for Belhaven for years. She has always lived on this land."

His mother sniffed and exchanged a knowing look with Grand-mère. "Well, it's not proper. It's a good thing we are here to protect your reputation."

"My reputation?" Max chuckled.

"From a social climber like that."

"Mother, I never thought you were such a snob. You and Father always welcomed friends of all ilk to our house."

His mother's lips thinned. "That was on the continent. It's different here at home, and you now have the title."

Max was disappointed in her attitude. His parents had always filled their house with guests for lavish parties—artists, politicians, lords and ladies, famous actors. His mother loved to entertain, and she developed friendships every new place his father had been sent. Max wasn't sure what this new attitude was about, but he wasn't pleased.

"Mother, Henry and Olivia had been friends since childhood. It makes sense that their close friendship would turn into love. I know she is still mourning her husband. I would think that is something you could sympathize with."

His mother's blue eyes softened, and her mouth relaxed from its disproving frown. She ran a shaky hand down her skirt, smoothing out invisible wrinkles. "All I'm saying is it's improper for her to live here still."

Max nodded. "She and I have discussed this, and she is

figuring out her next steps. Henry left her a sizable portion. She does not care for London, so she may settle somewhere close by as she has many friends in this community. I'm certainly not going to kick her out before Christmas. She was once my friend as well." Max knew his voice rose as he spoke. All the women looked startled by his tone. He couldn't help but defend Olivia. She had no one else to do so.

Grand-mère was the first to speak. "Of course, you shouldn't abruptly eject her from her home." She sent a narrow look to his mother. "We are here now as a buffer for respectability. I think we should all enjoy Christmastide and worry about the details later. She seems very nice, dear."

"I think it sounds romantic, childhood friends to lovers." Ginny sighed.

Max's heart ached at her words. That should have been their story, his and Livvy's. *Damn you, Henry, for stealing her away and for dying and leaving her alone with a broken heart.*

Chapter Fifteen

"THANK YOU, MRS. Peabody. You have been a gem preparing the house for Lord Rivenhall's family," Olivia said to her housekeeper as they finished up their morning meeting.

"My pleasure, my lady. I will have to bring on help for the kitchen now that I'm not just cooking for you. I was thinking of Mrs. Buxley's niece. She is young but has her aunt's talent in the kitchen."

Olivia nodded. "I defer to your judgment. One more thing, Lord Rivenhall's mother would like to throw a Christmas Eve dinner party to introduce him to local society." She grimaced. The party was the only thing Mrs. Drake and her daughters talked about at dinner last night. She had a terrible feeling it would be much grander than the intimate dinner party she had envisioned when she suggested it. Even Mr. Galey had betrayed her and enthusiastically agreed that a party was an excellent idea. "Please accommodate whatever she needs for the party. I would like to have as little to do with it as possible."

Mrs. Peabody's expression was neutral and professional, but there was an excited gleam in her eye. Olivia suspected that her housekeeper missed the frivolity of Christmas at Belhaven. "Yes, milady. I will take care of it."

"Thank you, Mrs. Peabody. I think that is all for this morning."

She rose as Mrs. Peabody left and wandered over to her chair by the window. It was clear and cold outside. It had snowed overnight, adding several inches to the ground. Condensation fogged the windowpane, and she drew the shape of a small dove with her finger. She should take the sleigh and go to the bookstore to continue her reorganization efforts. But she wasn't in the mood. Perhaps she should just snuggle up here and read. She didn't have to face the world if she never left her rooms. She sighed; who was she fooling? She was avoiding Max, her feelings, and her fears about what to do with herself after the new year. The first she could avoid by staying in her room, but the other two were harder to avoid. Later this afternoon, her friends would be coming by to discuss the new letters, and she was looking forward to the distraction.

Until then, she would not hide. Olivia turned and squared her shoulders. She would simply go downstairs and check on her guests. She was still the lady of the house, for now anyway, and she would not neglect her duties as hostess. Smoothing her hair, she reached for the doorknob and exited the room. Halfway down the corridor, the door to one of the linen closets was open. Olivia approached and peeked around the wooden door. Max stepped out of the closet at the same moment. She let out an embarrassing squeak of surprise.

"Max, what in heaven's name are you doing in the closet?"

His trademark grin spread wide. He held up his hands, displaying several pairs of ice-skating blades. "I am taking my sisters skating this morning. Care to join us?"

"No." She crossed her arms in front of her chest. Ice-skating with Max? No, too many fond memories. Too dangerous for her heart.

"Come along. It will be fun." The warmth of his smile lit his whole face. His eyes glowed with mischief and the promise of fun. He jiggled the blades. "I found four pairs."

She shook her head even though she was tempted. Damn him and his charming smile.

Max shrugged. "Well, I suppose you can stay here and help my mother and grandmother plan the Christmas Eve party. They did inquire about your whereabouts this morning at breakfast."

Olivia swallowed hard. Double damn. "Fine. Skating it is. I will need to change into something warmer."

"We will wait for you downstairs in the foyer. Don't look so grim. Don't you remember how much fun it is to watch me make a fool of myself on the ice? I look like a geriatric penguin."

Oliva turned on her heel before he could see her smile. Back inside her room, she added warm wool stockings under her skirts and layered on a knit sweater before donning her half-boots. She headed downstairs and was met by three identical smiles. There was no doubt of their familial status. All three siblings shared wide full-lipped mouths, sharp cheekbones, and golden eyes. Max and his sisters were already in coats, fur-lined capes, gloves, and muffs. Olivia joined them, and Mr. Daniels appeared at her elbow with her cape, fur-lined bonnet, gloves, and muff.

Outside, the sleigh was waiting, and they piled in. Foot bricks placed on the floor and blankets piled in one corner all waited to keep them warm. It was cold, but there was no wind, the perfect day for skating. The coachman flicked the reins, and they moved forward across the snow-covered lawns. It had been ages since she had been ice-skating. She had to admit a small flurry of excitement swirled in her belly. The pond was on the west side of the property near her old house. Mr. Johnson and his family lived on the other side of the pond, and he farmed the fields surrounding it. He had seven children and took it upon himself to monitor the thickness of the ice. He always tacked up a painted wood sign that marked the pond safe to skate.

"Did you ask Mr. Daniels if he knew that the pond was safe to skate?" she asked Max.

"No, should I have?"

"Mr. Johnson always monitors the ice to make sure it's thick enough to skate safely. Often in December, it can be too thin." Olivia glanced at his sisters. "We'll be able to tell when we arrive. He always posts a sign with a painting of an ice-skating bear on it when the ice is thick enough."

"An ice-skating bear?" Ginny laughed. "How funny."

The sleigh whooshed over the snow-covered fields. Olivia enjoyed the view. Most of Belhaven's land was green fields. It did not have the heavily wooded forests that Charlotte's family's estate sat on. Nor any of the gently rolling fields of lavender that was the hallmark of Weston's smaller estate. Belhaven traditionally grew hay and grazed sheep. The whole of Hertfordshire was blessed with fertile soil that was good for growing just about any crop.

The estate had a sizable apple orchard, and she raised bees and sold the honey locally. She had thought perhaps they should diversify by growing barley or even potatoes. Breweries had been popping up all across the county, including Lucius Grisham's place. But she hadn't the courage to rock the boat too much. After all, hay and sheep had kept the estate profitable for hundreds of years.

"Is all this land yours, Max?" Louisa asked.

Max glanced over at Olivia, and she nodded. "Yes, we are still on Belhaven land. The estate spans from the east side of Marbury. Marbury itself belongs to the Earl of Dearborn, whose home estate lies to the south of town. Belhaven has two smaller villages on its land. Your property ends at the county border to Essex."

Both sister's eyes grew round at her explanation. Max tugged on the collar of his coat as though he was having trouble swallowing. "Well, there you have it."

She took pity on him and offered a small smile. "Don't worry; we will discuss all the estate details and its holdings before we meet with Mr. Bromley on Friday. You have plenty of people that support you."

He nodded, but a furrow remained between his eyebrows as he stared out at the scenery. Olivia needed to remember that Max had not expected to become Earl of Rivenhall and that he knew very little about his inheritance. Everyone had expected her and Henry to have produced an heir. But their relationship had not been carnal in nature, and Henry refused to bow to society's expectations. He always knew that he would pass the title to Max. Unfortunately, he never had the opportunity to discuss this with his cousin. Olivia didn't know what had caused the rift between the two men, just that Max had never responded to any of Henry's letters.

Why had Max cut his friends so cruelly out of his life? The need to know burned in her gut. She had lived for his letters filled with the minutia of his day and how much he missed her. She had immediately regretted not going with him when he asked, but her father would have never allowed it. Then the letters had stopped. Each Thursday she would wait anxiously on the bench in front of the house for her father to return from Marbury with the post. And each week her father would shake his head. Nothing for her. All those letters written with her whole heart had gone unanswered.

Olivia glanced again over at Max. He caught her gaze and winked. How could he act so charming, so kind, when he had broken her heart? Did he regret it? Or did he just need her knowledge of the estate? Would he shuffle her off in the new year once he settled into his new role?

Her thoughts buzzed around like her bees when they

swarmed to protect their queen. She must protect her heart; it could not bear another blow. The past was better left in the past. Getting the answers to her questions would only cause her pain. Olivia sucked in a deep breath of frosty air. *Stop overthinking and just have fun today.*

"Lady Rivenhall, look, I see the sign! The ice-skating bear." Ginny's excited exclamation pulled Olivia from her thoughts.

"Excellent. And please, call me Olivia," she replied.

The sleigh came to a stop, and Max stepped out first. He helped each of his sisters down to the frozen ground. Last was Olivia, and she reluctantly took his hand. Even through their gloves she could feel the heat of him. He didn't let go but instead tucked her hand into the crook of his arm to lead her over to the wooden bench where they could don their blades.

"Look there are children skating already!" Louisa pointed to the pond.

Sure enough, Mr. Johnson's children skated on the ice. Their father stood watching from the other side. He waved when he spotted them. Olivia waved back with a smile. She looked up at Max. "Mr. Johnson farms the land around this pond. Just as his father did before him. His wife not only has given birth to seven children but is also the local midwife. They are excellent tenants."

Max nodded, and they both watched as Mr. Johnson made his way around the pond toward them. Kit, their coachman, knelt to help strap blades onto the girls' boots.

They must have skated before because they didn't hesitate to walk over on wobbly feet and skate onto the ice. Ginny and Louisa grasped hands and glided away. Once they were in the middle, Ginny stopped and spun her sister around her in a wide circle. Louisa pointed her toes wide and leaned into the spin. Laughter spilled from her lips.

"They are certainly better than you ever were," Olivia commented.

"They lived in Prussia for four years. There is nothing but winter activities to do."

Olivia smirked. "Jealous?"

Max stepped closer to her. His voice was like warm honey. "Perhaps you can hold my hand and lead me around. I'll gladly take any assistance you are willing to give."

"Oh no. It's far too entertaining to see you wobble around like…what did you call yourself? A geriatric penguin."

Max put a hand to his chest as though she had wounded him, but before he could reply, she spotted Mr. Johnson striding toward them. Olivia gave Max an elbow in his side. "Good morning, Mr. Johnson."

"Good morning, Lady Rivenhall." The man tipped his wool cap. "I haven't seen you come skating in a long while."

"True enough. Let me introduce you to the new Lord Rivenhall." She looked up at Max. "This is Mr. Johnson, one of our very best tenants."

"Good morning, Lord Rivenhall. I had a feeling you w the new lord. Betsy heard the news from Mrs. Kirk."

"It's a pleasure to meet you, Mr. Johnson," Max replied.

"How is your wife?" Olivia asked.

"Busy. She delivered Mrs. George's baby just last night, and Mrs. Haden birthed a fine son just last week." He frowned. "She is worried for the pair, though. Mr. Haden has not returned yet, and she said they are running low on firewood."

"Mr. Haden is a seaman and travels many months during the year. Mrs. Haden lives in the village with her mother-in-law," Olivia explained to Max.

"We will have a cart of wood sent over to her right away," Max said.

Mr. Johnson's eyes widened. "Good, good. It will set my wife's mind at ease. Are those your daughters, my lord?" he pointed to the girls.

"No, my younger sisters. I'm not married as of yet, much to my mother's dismay."

Mr. Johnson chuckled. "It was nice to meet you, Lord Rivenhall. Have fun skating." He tipped his hat again and strolled away.

"That was very generous." Olivia turned to Max. His immediate offer had surprised her as well. It was nothing less than what she would have done, but the decisive action spoke volumes about how Max already thought of his position as caretaker of this land and its tenants.

"We can't let people freeze to death." He shrugged his shoulders.

She tilted her head up to assess his expression of what

looked to be forced nonchalance. "I know you are overwhelmed by the prospect of being Rivenhall, and you have a lot to learn, but you have good instincts. I think you'll do well in your new role." She patted his arm. "Come on, let's skate."

"No, I think I shall just watch."

Olivia sat down on the bench, and Kit rushed over with the remaining two pairs of blades. "Don't be silly," she said. "You promised me I could watch you make a fool of yourself. Sit down and let Kit strap on your blades."

Max sighed but sat down and waited for Kit to cinch the leather straps tightly around his boots. They stood and cautiously clomped down to the pond's edge. A large tree grew there. Above them its thick gnarled branches stretched out over the ice. Olivia stepped onto the ice first. Finding her balance, she gave a push and glided out onto the main part of the pond. Max's sisters skated over.

"Olivia! This is wonderful. What a nice pond to skate on," Ginny exclaimed.

Olivia smiled. "I haven't skated in ages." She pushed out again and enjoyed the cold air against her cheeks as she gained some speed. She executed a spin, and the world whirled by in a blur of white. Louisa and Ginny clapped. Olivia came to a stop and gave a little curtsy. When she looked up, she saw Max still standing in the snow on the side of the pond. She skated forward. "Come on out. I promise to help you."

He shook his head. His sisters skated toward him and

echoed what she'd said, beckoning him to come onto the ice. Max stepped one foot onto the ice, wobbled almost losing his balance, then managed to get both feet balanced. He grinned.

Olivia held out a hand. "Now, just skate slowly to me."

He moved one foot forward, lost his balance, and in a desperate attempt to stay upright, grabbed hold of a low tree branch above him. The branch shook as it took his weight and all the snow clinging to it tumbled onto Max's head and no doubt down the collar of his coat. The expression of shock on his face was priceless. Olivia clapped a gloved hand over her mouth to stifle her chuckle, but Max's sisters had no such compunction; they howled with laughter.

Max ripped off his hat and shook the snow off. He gave his sisters a dark look as he brushed snow from his shoulders. Olivia took pity and skated up directly in front of him. Once he had his hat back in place, she took hold of his hands and slowly skated backward, pulling him along.

"I don't know how I let them talk me into this," he muttered. He gripped her fingers tightly as he shuffled along.

"Because you are a good big brother," Olivia replied. "You were never an excellent skater, but I do remember you being able to at least stay on your feet."

"It's been ten years since I have skated. I'm rusty." He grimaced as they hit an uneven part, and he tripped a little. "Besides, Henry was as terrible as me, so it never mattered if the two of us tumbled around like drunks on the ice. Half of the time, we pushed each other down on purpose just to embarrass the other in front of you."

Olivia raised an eyebrow. "Did you now?"

Max grinned again, and she was glad to see his good humor return. "Henry never skated anymore. He said that married men did not ice-skate; that it was only for foolish bachelors looking to impress the ladies. He always stood on the side smoking with the other married men."

Max's smile disappeared. He let go of one of her hands, and they turned to move across the ice side by side. Still moving slowly as Max's movements were stiff and stilted. They had made a whole loop around the pond before Max spoke again. "I am still struggling to come to terms that the two of you were married."

"Perhaps if you had replied to any of Henry's letters, you would have come to the wedding and seen for yourself." Olivia felt the old bitterness rise in her throat. Max's abandonment had not only hurt her but Henry as well.

"I couldn't."

"Couldn't be bothered, you mean." She dropped his hand.

Max grabbed it back, holding it in a tight grip. "No. I couldn't. I couldn't watch you pledge yourself to him." His eyes flashed with fire. "I couldn't bear that your heart could belong to another."

Olivia froze at his tortured words. She opened her mouth and closed it again. Why would he even have cared after leaving them without a word for two years? He was the one who had severed their friendship, their dreams for a future together.

"Olivia, come skate with me." Louisa slid up next to them, followed by her sister.

"Yes, Louisa wants you to show her how to spin," Ginny said. "I'll stay and babysit Max."

Louisa reached for her hand. "How do you spin without getting dizzy and falling over?"

"Not now, Louisa," Max growled. His grip tightened on Olivia's hand, and he tried to move his body between her and Louisa. Then Max lost his footing. His arm swung in a wide circle as he tried to catch his balance. He twisted around and gripped Olivia's waist. His momentum pushed her off-balance as well, and her right foot slipped out from under her. They executed a strange slow-motion dance movement before tumbling to the ice. Max's arm wrapped around her at the last minute, and he took the brunt of the fall with her landing on top of him.

"Oh my! Are you two hurt?" Ginny exclaimed.

Olivia couldn't answer. All her breath had been knocked from her lungs in the fall. She raised her head and stared down at Max's face.

He grimaced. "Sorry. You all right?"

Olivia nodded. She sucked in a deep breath slowly through her nose, filling her lungs back up. "Yes. You?"

His eyes twinkled. "You are in my arms. I'm not complaining." He squeezed her waist where his arm still banded around her.

Olivia felt her face flush hot. Max's lean hard body

pressed against hers from shoulder to thigh. How would it feel to be this close unencumbered with all these layers of clothing? Somewhere private where she could run her hands across his muscled chest and press her lips to his throat right where his pulse raced. She stared at the spot hidden by his cravat. Would the skin be smooth or scratchy with stubble?

Max's lips inches from hers, curled up into a slow smile as though he knew exactly what she was thinking. He was incorrigible! She pushed against his chest to lever up, and he grunted.

"Oh, sorry!" She scrambled off him to her knees.

Ginny held out a hand to help her get to her feet. "Thank you," Olivia said as she brushed snow from her skirts.

Max lay on the ice staring up at the sky.

"Max, aren't you going to get up?" Louisa asked him.

"No, I'll never manage it. This is my life now. Promise you'll come to visit me when I'm a snowman."

The girls giggled. Olivia shook her head and held out a hand. "Come on. We'll help you."

Ginny also offered her hand, and between the two of them, they managed to get Max to his feet. He looked longingly at the bank. "Ginny, would you be a dear and get me to dry land so I can take these blasted things off?"

Olivia watched him shuffle slowly across the pond as he held onto his sister's arm. She chuckled. He really did look like a geriatric penguin.

Chapter Sixteen

OLIVIA SIPPED HER tea while her friends chatted around her. The library was always their meeting spot, the coziest room at Belhaven. Situated on the second floor of one of the turrets, it had an odd octagonal shape. But Henry had shelves custom built in to house her book collection, and she had chosen upholstered chairs that were made for comfort to create a seating area in the middle. The room's one window was tall and narrow, soaring up eight feet and bringing in much-needed sunlight on this winter afternoon. Opposite the window, a fire roared cheerfully in a Pantheon stove.

She couldn't concentrate on the conversation around her. Instead, her mind kept rolling over Max's comments from earlier at the pond. As much as she had decided to focus on her future and not dwell on their past, she increasingly needed to know why Max had severed their friendship so callously. A long while ago, she had come to terms with the fact that Max had moved on to more exciting things—that their feelings had just been a product of adolescent infatuation. But his words today seem to belie all those assumptions.

Blast it. She was doing it again, mooning over Maxwell

Drake! Analyzing every comment, overthinking every interaction. No more. She needed to get Max out of her system. The trouble was that his presence was frying her wits every time he was near. She couldn't stop thinking about kissing his full lips, exploring that broad muscled chest, and tasting his tanned skin. He was an all too handsome distraction, to be sure. Olivia huffed out a frustrated breath.

"What's wrong? You don't like the idea of reading aloud?" Charlotte asked.

Olivia blinked and forced herself to concentrate on her friends' conversation. "Pardon? Sorry, I wasn't paying attention."

"I was just saying that we should read the new letters aloud as opposed to passing them around," Charlotte said.

"But who is brave enough to read aloud? We all know how explicit some of the letters can be." Eleanor blushed.

"I will," Olivia offered. She had already read them with Max, and they didn't contain anything racy; in fact, they were rather sad. She picked up a letter.

My dearest love,

Your letter tore my heart from my chest. I cannot bear the thought that you would marry another, that you have no choice in the matter. Your words of love are little balm for my soul when I know you are trapped in a life you do not choose. I berate myself every day that I am not the man you need me to be. My soldier's pension barely keeps the roof over my mother's head, and only the talent of my prose allows me enough to feed and clothe myself. Mrs. T's good recommendation might afford me my next commission, but alas, I can't give you the life you are used to, the life you deserve. I feel that I am drowning in the stormy sea, our love a ship that is lost to me, growing smaller and smaller on the horizon.

Yours always, J

Olivia laid down the letter on the table. "I feel as though we are eavesdropping on his pain and desperation. Poor man."

Susanna sniffled. "He is giving up on them. I can feel it."

"But they do see each other again. The other letter tells of when he sees her at a London party with the man she is to marry. He speaks of his jealousy and asks her to leave her window open to let him visit her at night," Sophia said.

Susanna pouted. "I can't believe you ruined the letter before I could read it."

"We wanted to find out the name on the address. It was the only way," Charlotte said.

Susanna reached across and slid the charcoaled letter toward her. "It was very clever of Mr. Drake," she conceded. "I'm still the only one who hasn't met him."

"He is very handsome and strong." Charlotte's eyes twinkled with mischief. "He was holding Olivia in his arms when Daniel and I came into the store."

"What?" Ellie sat forward, her mouth agape.

Olivia sent Charlotte a glare. "He caught me when I

tripped on the stairs. Simply that."

Charlotte let out a long hum. "There was nothing simple about the smoldering look you two were sharing."

"Can we focus back on the letters, please?" Olivia said. The last thing she wanted to talk about was Max.

Ellie cleared her throat. She glanced around the circle. "I have been keeping something from you all." Reaching into the top of her bodice, she pulled out a folded piece of parchment. "There was another letter from the batch Lucius and I found in London." A collective gasp came from around the table. "I didn't want to show you this one because I believe it marks the end of their relationship. And now that we've discovered it is Daniel and Miles's aunt, we know the lovers do not have a happy ending." She sighed and unfolded the parchment. "Truly, I held it back in order to not dash your hopes for the couple."

Olivia's heart sank. "Read it. We must know even if it's not as we hoped."

Ellie nodded.

"*Dearest Diana,*

We have been found out. Your father came to see me. His anger was understandable. I have stolen your affection and have not a way to make an honest woman out of you. Your loving words and the memories of our stolen moments together have sustained me through some very hard times this past year. But I am beholden to my patroness, and as your father reminded me, you are far above my station. I must end our affair here and now. This is not easy to write, but I believe this is the right path. Please know how much I have loved you. Never doubt that. But the world is more complicated than you and me alone.

Love, J"

"No-ooo," Susanna wailed.

Ellie reached over a squeezed her hand. "That's just how I felt. But I so hoped that there would be more, that in the end, they would find a way to be together."

Olivia slumped back against her chair. Her friends mirrored her pose. The silence stretched as they each came to terms with the sad ending to the mysterious love letters. But that was life, wasn't it? Life didn't always work out the way you envisioned. People disappointed you. People you loved left. They died.

"Diana married the man her parents chose, I assume?" Sophia asked.

Charlotte nodded. "Yes, Diana was married to Viscount Wells. She was widowed young and has not chosen to remarry. Daniel said he does not remember much about her husband; he and Miles were still young when he died."

"Perhaps she never stopped loving her secret lover," Susanna said.

"Perhaps she simply didn't want another husband." Sophia smirked.

Sophia was a widow as well. Although she never spoke of

her husband. Even her closest friends knew very little about her life in Italy. The book club members never pried, hoping that one day Sophia would trust them enough to speak about her past. Olivia had the sense that her marriage had been unhappy and Sophia had come to England for a new beginning. Sophia was wealthy, but she lived simply in her own house in the village.

Charlotte bit her lip. "Do you think we should speak with Diana? I feel guilty about having her letters. They should be returned to her, don't you agree?"

Olivia nodded. "Yes. The letters are hers."

Everyone around the table nodded their agreement. "Aunt Diana and Miles are arriving in two days to spend Christmastide with us," Charlotte said.

"Do you think she would tell us about him?" Susanna asked.

"It may be too painful for her to talk about. After all, it obviously ended badly," Olivia said.

"But it was so long ago," Susanna replied.

"The past can still be painful. Despite the saying, time does not heal all wounds," Olivia said. She still felt the pain of Max's abandonment.

She remembered acutely the disappointment which had filled her chest every time the post came, and no letter from him had arrived. And that disappointment had turned to panic when her father informed her of the marriage he had arranged. She had sent a last desperate missive to both Max and Henry asking for help. Henry had been the one to show up at her door. He had been the one to listen to her frustrations with her father's orders and her tears over Max's silence. Yes, pain, even old wounds, had a way of sticking with you.

"I can speak with her privately and ask her if she is willing to tell us about it. But I can't promise anything," Charlotte said. "She is a second mother to Daniel and Miles and I won't do anything to cause her hurt."

"Yes, of course." Ellie gave Susanna a quelling look when she opened her mouth to protest.

Susanna was the most impetuous of all of them and it often got her into trouble. But she was also fearless, straightforward, and the sort of friend who would help you bury the body without asking any questions.

Olivia laughed outright at Susanna's mulish expression. "Let's change the topic of conversation. You all are invited to a Christmas Eve dinner here at Belhaven Hall."

"Lovely!" Ellie exclaimed.

"We are happy to attend. But I thought you were boycotting Christmas festivities this year?" Charlotte asked.

Olivia grimaced. "Drake—I mean Rivenhall's entire family has come to visit for the holiday." She cocked an eyebrow. "They adore throwing parties, and they adore Christmas, so here we are having a party to introduce him to the local quality. My job is to invite the right people." She shot her friends a smile. "So, I intend to make sure it's intimate. Charlotte, your whole household is invited of course, and don't worry I will not invite your parents."

Charlotte sighed. "My mother will be beside herself if she doesn't get to meet the new Rivenhall. You should just invite them. Besides, my brother Edward and his family are in residence at Markham House for the holidays, and I do feel bad for Katherine having to manage my mother all alone."

"All right, I will invite them as well. I'd hoped to get through the season with as little fanfare as possible, but Max and his family love Christmas." She rolled her eyes.

"You used to as well, my dear," Ellie said. "Belhaven always had the most fabulous Twelfth Night parties."

The other ladies exchanged looks across the table.

"That was always Henry." Olivia swallowed around the lump that formed in her throat. "I don't know how to do this without him."

Sophia wrapped an arm around her shoulders. "With your friends by your side."

Chapter Seventeen

MAX ENJOYED THE ride into Marbury. He was beginning to adapt to the cold, or at least remember to dress warmer. His trousers had a warm woolen lining and he had on sheepskin-lined gloves, and his wool knit cap. The ladies rode in the sleigh, wrapped in capes with fur blankets on their laps, and hot bricks at their feet. The sky was clear and blue. It would be a perfect day to browse the holiday market.

He was grateful to be on his horse and away from the constant chatter of the women in his family. The constant banter could be cheerful and exhausting all at once. Max found that he had missed being with those few people who knew him well. With his family he didn't have to be on guard, to constantly analyze his environment or every nuance of the conversation. He hadn't felt this relaxed in years.

He slowed the horse's pace to match the sleigh as they entered the town. "This is Marbury. It's a charming town. Lots of shops, a coaching inn, and a new brewery just opened."

His mother sniffed derisively, but her sharp eyes took in everything as they rolled into town. Louisa and Ginny craned their necks to glance up and down the streets they passed. The coachman pulled to a stop at the square in the middle of town. Max dismounted and strode over to help his grandmother from the conveyance. Then he handed down his mother and sisters.

"Look at all the tents! There must be at least two dozen," Ginny said.

Kit tied Max's horse to the back of the sleigh. "When should I come back for you, my lord?"

"Perhaps in an hour? Would that be enough time, ladies?" Max asked.

His mother nodded. "Yes, any longer, and we'll turn into icicles."

Max gave Kit a shilling. "After you take care of the horses, get yourself a lager to warm up."

"Thank you, sir." Kit tipped his hat with a smile. Then he jumped back onto the box and snapped the reins.

Ginny and Louisa each slipped a hand through Grandmère's arms, flanking her as they headed down the first aisle of tents. Max offered his arm to his mother, and they followed at a slower pace. Louisa and Ginny pulled Grandmère from booth to booth, but his mother spent time assessing the wares at each tent carefully.

After perusing a selection of nuts, she ordered two bags of walnuts and three bags of almonds. Max paid the vendor, and they strolled again. "It's nice to spend time with you, Maxie," his mother said. "Even if we did have to chase you all the way to England."

"It is nice to spend time with you all as well. This inheritance came at exactly the right time. Italy was dangerous, and I don't think I will return any time soon."

"Were you able to procure the Vasari?" she asked.

He nodded. "But I was ambushed en route to the sale. The painting was taken."

His mother shook her head. "There is no honor among thieves anymore."

Max glanced over at her scowling face. He patted her arm. "Well, that is all over for me. Now I can afford to pay for whatever you need."

She nodded. "Yes, this is a boon for our family. Your new title will give us the opportunities your father always craved for you all. You know that he always did whatever he could to give you three the best life."

"Yes, of course, Mother," he agreed automatically. Max knew his father had been motivated by greed. No amount of money had filled his need to have more. He had often expressed his bitterness at having the bad luck of being the younger brother, at having to work for a living. But Max kept his thoughts to himself.

Max glanced ahead to where his sister oohed and ahhed over a table of beaded earrings. His father's side business had afforded them a pampered upbringing. If his mother wanted to romanticize what he and his father had done fencing stolen goods then he would let her. The last thing he wanted was to tell his mother he had almost died in a Venetian gutter.

"I've been wanting to speak about Lady Rivenhall," his mother said. "Don't think I haven't noticed the way you look at her."

Max stiffened. "I don't know what you mean."

She patted his arm. "She is lovely and very amiable. I can understand your attraction. Is she the one you used to write to when you were younger?"

"Yes, we used to be friends."

His mother shot him a look from under her lashes. "Just remember she is the widow of your cousin. Now that you are the Earl of Rivenhall, you need to live by the rules of society. Just keep that in mind, Max."

Max frowned. He didn't need his mother to remind him that Olivia was his cousin's widow. He was all too aware that she mourned another man. "I just want to bring her some Christmas cheer. Henry died right before Christmas last year, and she is having trouble envisioning the holiday without him. In fact, so am I. I spent many Christmastide here with Henry. I cannot believe he is gone."

"I understand. Just be careful, my dear," his mother warned.

They joined the rest of the family as the ladies looked over a table full of ribbons. Max stood patiently with his hands behind his back as the merits of various colors were debated heatedly by his sisters. He glanced down the row to see what else was part of the market. Across from them, he spotted a table full of small barrels of sweets and wandered over. Sugared nuts, crackled toffee, and jellies of all sorts vied for attention besides colorful marzipan cut into fanciful shapes. The sweet smells of sugar and almonds permeated the air.

The woman behind the table smiled warmly. "Can I help you, sir?"

"Hmmm, yes. Can I get a bag of the orange jellies?"

"Certainly." She took a tin scoop and filled a small burlap sack with the jellies. Then she tied it closed with a bright red ribbon before handing it to him.

Max paid her and tucked the bag into the pocket of his coat. When he turned, his family had moved on to the next tent. This one sold filigree boxes of various sizes. Snuff boxes, cigar boxes, and larger ones for writing supplies covered the table. Ginny and Louisa huddled over one section and when he stepped toward them to see what they looked at, the girls spun around to shoo him away. "Max, go away. How are we to surprise you if you act as our shadow?"

Max held up his hands and backed away, happy to go wander around. At the end of the row, a large tent housed stacks and stacks of fresh greenery. The spicy smell of balsam drew him down toward the display. Wreaths and beribboned lengths of garland hung from hooks attached to the tent poles, and balls of mistletoe hung with twine from the ceiling of the tent.

His grandmother came to stand next to him. "It smells heavenly in here," Grand-mère announced. "We should get some to decorate the Hall."

Max fingered a bough of soft evergreen with bright red

holly berries and mistletoe nestled into its woven branches. Perhaps if he hung it up at Belhaven, he could steal a kiss from Olivia. He knew his mother was right about how he couldn't keep his eyes off of Livvy. The sane thing would be to keep his distance until she moved out from Belhaven. He needed to be careful not to risk his heart again on a woman who loved another. But kissing Olivia had infected his blood with her taste. He wanted more, far too much more.

The seller approached—a heavy-set man in a bright red jacket. "Can I help you to select anything?"

Max glanced over at his grandmother, who nodded. He turned back to the man. "Yes, we'll take it all."

The man's mouth fell open. He stuttered for a moment before replying. "All?"

"Yes, have it delivered to Belhaven Hall. Except for these," he pointed to the balsam bough and a wreath, "and that garland there. I will take those with me."

"Yes, Lord Rivenhall. I'll have everything delivered this afternoon."

"Excellent." Max paid the man without haggling. Another benefit of his new inheritance, he would never have to haggle over price again. Max gathered up the greenery in his arms. "Sir, can you send someone to the inn with a message for my coachman Kit. Tell him I plan to stay in town longer, and that he should leave my horse at the stables when he comes to fetch the ladies."

"Yes, sir." The man snapped his fingers, and a young boy sitting in the back of the tent jumped up. "My son will go immediately."

"And where are you going off to?" His mother's voice rang out.

Max turned to find the rest of his family behind him. "I have a special delivery to make."

Four sets of eyebrows rose high. Max just chuckled. "Time to spread some Christmas cheer. Have fun. Purchase whatever you want. I'll see you back at the Hall." He leaned over to buss his grandmother's cheek and then his mother's, ignoring her sharp look of disapproval. Then Max whistled "Deck the Halls" as he strode up the main street toward the bookshop.

Chapter Eighteen

OLIVIA LEANED HER chin on one hand and sighed as she sat behind Mr. Buxley's desk. She glanced around at the shop's bookshelves, dust-free and organized by topic. Thanks to her friends' help, they had spent the last four days reorganizing the shop. This morning, Olivia had dusted and polished every wood surface. She flipped open her watch pin, one o'clock in the afternoon, and not a single customer had entered the shop all day. How exactly did Mr. Buxley stay in business?

She had a fair idea that she and her book club were Mr. Buxley's best customers, but surely there were other patrons of the shop? Where were the newspaper readers? Or the customers in need of a fresh supply of writing paper? The display of paper, quills, and charcoal pencils was quite nice, even if it was tucked away in the back corner. Olivia straightened her shoulders. Well, she would just have to spread the word that the bookshop had new management. Perhaps she could sponsor some sort of event here to let people see how pleasant it could be to shop.

The front door opened, and Olivia looked over eagerly. *A customer!* But it was just Max, his arms so full of greenery she could only see the red tip of his nose and his gray wool hat. He used his foot to slam the door shut behind him, and as he lowered his arms his toothy smile emerged from behind the greenery.

Olivia stood. "What have you got there?"

"Decoration for the shop. I thought we could liven up the window." He shrugged his wide shoulders.

Olivia crossed her arms in front of her chest. "I specifically said I do not want to partake in Christmas frivolities this year."

Max glance around the empty shop. "And how many shoppers have you had today?"

Olivia gritted her teeth. "None."

"Perhaps a decorated window would attract some customers. It would at least tell people the shop was open for business. Had Mr. Buxley ever decorated the window before?"

"No, I don't think he ever has."

"Perhaps it will make people curious." He shifted his weight from one foot to the other and adjusted the greenery in his arms.

"Come and put that all down here on the desk. What did you do, buy out the entire booth?"

Max set down his armload on the desk with a relieved sigh. "Actually, I did. The rest is being delivered to Belhaven this afternoon." He whipped off his hat, and his cheeks flushed matching his red nose.

Olivia's mouth dropped open. Hadn't he listened to anything she'd said about not wanting to celebrate Christmas? Of all the high-handed... She slowly inhaled a deep breath. She needed to remember Belhaven was no longer her house. It belonged to Max, and he could do whatever he wanted with it, decorate it for Christmas, or burn it down to the ground if he so chose.

But the bookshop was hers, or least it may be hers if Mr. Buxley agreed to sell it to her. As much as she wished to kick Max and his Christmas cheer out of the shop, she had a sinking feeling he was right. Decorating the window might attract attention of a few paying customers. "Do as you please then. I have things to take care of."

She turned on her heel and strode to the back. Coming to a stop in front of the back wall, she stared at the shelves. She had no earthly idea what things she could take care of, but Max didn't have to know that. Olivia randomly pulled a book from the travel section. *A Gentleman's Guide to Traveling in Austria.* Turning sideways, she opened it and flipped through the pages while watching Max from the corner of her eye. First, he organized the pile of greenery, separating what she could see was a long garland, a wreath, and a bough dotted with red holly berries. Then he removed his greatcoat and unwound the scarf from his neck, setting them both on a nearby chair. Next, he stood in front of the window, its many panes of glass showering him with sunshine. His arms crossed and his jacket pulled tight across his broad shoulders. Olivia bit her bottom lip and marveled had how changed he was from the lanky boy of his youth. Wide muscled shoulders covered by a fitted navy jacket tapered to a lean waist, then to a firm backside and muscled thighs that filled out his gray wool trousers nicely.

What was she doing? She shouldn't be thinking about his thighs or his backside. She also shouldn't be wondering how silky his hair would be if she ran her fingers through it. She turned back to stare at the bookshelf. *Well, why not?* She argued with herself. She was not married, and she was not a blasted nun. She could admire a man's physique if she wanted to. She was twenty-six years old and still had not sampled passion with a man. Why not Max? *You know why not. Too many old feelings tangled up with him.* She sighed.

"Do you think Mr. Buxley has some tools around here?" Max's voice startled her. "I'll need some tacks."

She whirled around. Max stood in the opening between the two rooms. "Did you check in the closet behind the desk?"

Max shook his head. "Thanks."

He strode over and opening the closet door, he disappeared inside. "Could you hand me a lamp, please?" His muffled voice called out from the closet's dim interior.

Olivia grabbed a lamp, walked over, and held it up to illuminate the walk-in closet.

"Thanks," Max said. He began to rummage through the shelves. As he bent over to look in the back, she received a very nice view. Her face heated, and she licked her lips. He certainly had one fine backside.

Max stood up, and when he swiveled around, he held a

hammer and a small box of tacks. His smile was triumphant. "Found some!"

Olivia backed away from the doorway to let him exit the closet. His proximity sent a sizzle through her. He smelled like the outdoors, like pine trees and fresh air. She took another large step back. Max came out into the shop and headed straight for the window, where he took one end of the garland in one hand and the hammer in the other. But when he tried to juggle holding a tack in place, he dropped the end of the garland. He bent over to pick it up, and Olivia realized she would never get her pulse back to normal if he kept that up.

She moved next to him. "Here, let me help you hold that."

"Thanks." Max handed her the garland.

"Here?" she held it up at one corner of the window.

"Yes, perfect." Max stepped behind her, his body only inches from her and his arm bracketing her head as he stretched up to hammer at a long tack to secure the end of the decoration. Goose bumps rose on her arms as his warm breath tickled her ear. In the next instant, he pulled back and reached for another section from the middle and draped it a third of the way across. "Hold, please."

Olivia slid down in front of him and did as he instructed. They tacked the pretty greenery all around the widow. She held her breath as he leaned in again to tack the last corner. Was it her imagination, or had he taken a large inhale before stepping back? Had he smelled her hair? Olivia swiveled to face him, staring up into his tawny eyes. His pupils were large, and his nostrils flared as he sucked in a long breath.

"Is that all?" she asked. Her voice came out too high-pitched and Olivia tore her gaze from his. "I have things to do."

Max strode back a few feet to assess the window. After a moment, he added some greenery to the display ledge right in front. Examining the window once more, Max let out a long "hmmmm," then turned and plucked some holly from the pile on the desk and inserted here and there into the garland.

"It looks quite nice," Olivia admitted.

"Perhaps some books to display in the window? What sort of book would people give as gifts?"

Olivia thought about the travel guide she had plucked from the shelf. "I've got some ideas." She headed back to the travel section to peruse the titles. She heard more hammering from behind her as she collected the titles she wanted. Perhaps a few novels as well. That's what she liked to read best. Setting her books on the table, she moved to the fiction section. Ahhh, Mrs. Radcliffe. Perfect. Who wouldn't want to sit by the fire and read a good mystery?

After carefully choosing three more mystery titles, Olivia gathered all seven books and returned to the front of the shop. She stopped short. The space smelled amazing; the sweet fresh scent of balsam boughs scented the air. Max had tacked up little bouquets of holly at the top of each section of shelves and placed more greenery, dotted with bright red berries, along the front of the desk. It was lovely and Christmas-y. Unexpected tears pressed against the back of her eyes. But these were not sad tears, rather they were happy tears. She had missed this, the simple pleasure of a room beautifully decorated for the holidays. It didn't hurt her heart, but rather, it buoyed it.

She brought the books to the display window and set each one up with covers facing out the window. Max picked up a travel guide to Italy and flipped through the pages, stopping to admire the drawings. Olivia glanced over at him.

"I thought perhaps with all this cold weather people might like to escape to a warmer climate and dream about the warm Mediterranean Sea."

"Good choice. I know I will be thinking about my little flat in Venice. The balcony looked out onto the sea. I would stand outside and let the warm salty breeze cleanse my soul." Max flushed. She wondered if he'd meant to say something so personal.

"What trouble did your soul get into while you lived in Italy?" She arched an eyebrow.

The red flush deepened. "Nothing. Nothing I would tell a lady anyway." He turned to set his book into the display.

"Will you miss your job? Now that you are living back in England?"

"No. Definitely not." He shook his head. "I enjoyed the hunt for missing pieces, but I did not enjoy the people I worked for or the means to which we had to go to obtain some of the paintings."

Olivia frowned. He was so cryptic about his work. She placed another book into the display. "Where else have you traveled? Tell me about somewhere warm."

Max smiled and leaned back against the desk. "I spent a year in Egypt. It's warm there all year-round. The desert sands are beautiful but deadly. Also, there are far too many French living there. Now India is much nicer. In the south, the weather is warm, and the local people warmer. I met many friends in the two years I lived there."

"Where is your favorite place that you have visited?"

He pursed his lips. "I suppose I would have to say Italy, but not Venice, farther south on the other side of the peninsula is a town where the houses are built right into the mountainside. Everyone can look out their windows and have a view of the deep blue sea."

"It sounds beautiful." Olivia pondered his descriptions. Perhaps she should travel to the continent. She would like to see a bit of the world. Maybe she could convince Sophia to be her traveling companion.

Max straightened. He reached out and brushed a finger down her cheek. "I wish we could have traveled there together. We would have explored the small winding streets, eaten olives and cheese and sweet figs. In the evenings, I would have held you in my arms on the terrace of our house and kissed each freckle that you gained from the hot Mediterranean sun. We would have been happy, I think."

Olivia's imagination ran wild with his description. Max leaned closer, and his head dipped, his gaze locked on her mouth. Her blood pulsed with the need for his kiss, for his fantasy. But an old scar ached in her chest. She stepped backward. "Instead, you left me behind."

"I asked you to go with me." His gaze swung up to meet hers, his eyes soft, filled with regret. "But things are different now. We are different." He reached out to cup her face.

Olivia shook her head. She moved away from him. She couldn't risk believing his sweet promises again. Her heart was too bruised. Oh, but she wanted to take a risk, to let him fold her into his arms and sweep her sensible thoughts away with a brush of his lips. *Foolish, she was so foolish.* She slapped her hand against the dark wood trim of the archway where she stood in the opening between the two rooms. "You never wrote." Her voice cracked with emotion. "You left me behind when I needed you."

Max's expression hardened; his jaw clenched. "We are going to talk about that false statement sometime soon." He prowled toward her, closing the distance between them. "But not now. Right now, I am going to kiss you under the mistletoe."

Olivia glanced up. Above them a ball of mistletoe and holly hung by a cheerful red ribbon.

His hand cupped the side of her face, and this time she didn't move away, ensnared by the heat burning in his eyes. "We shouldn't," she murmured. But the protest was weak, and she couldn't seem to muster any conviction behind her words. Instead, her traitorous hands came up to rest on his chest. His heartbeat was strong, his breathing fast and shallow.

Max's arm slid around her waist to pull her flush against him, erasing the space between them. His mouth possessed hers with hot, hungry lips. Olivia gasped at his passionate onslaught and Max's tongue dove between her parted lips. She melted, allowing his lips and tongue to tease, letting him stoke the flames of desire low in her belly into a wildfire. Max nipped at her lower lip, and one hand slid up to grasp the back of her neck. He tilted her head to pepper kisses across her cheek.

"Dear Lord, Livvy, you taste so sweet, even better than I remembered," he murmured into her ear. Then he took her earlobe into his mouth and sucked slowly.

A moan escaped her lips. His kisses, his words, the heat from his body radiating against her all stirred her desire into a frenzy. This was what she craved; this is what passion should feel like.

Max pulled back; his fingers gently kneaded the back of her neck. "Livvy, this, what's between us, has for me never changed. Perhaps we could begin fresh?" He bent and pressed another kiss against her lips. Soft and oh so tempting. "Just think about it."

Then he strode across the room to the desk and grabbed his greatcoat and hat. He turned and flashed her a wide smile before opening the door and exiting out into the cold afternoon. Olivia pressed a hand to her lips with trembling fingers. Max's kiss had unlocked something inside her she hadn't thought she would experience again. Desire raced through her veins making her feel alive, like her body had awoken from a long slumber. This feeling was reckless, glorious, terrifying. She wandered across the room to the desk, and ran her fingertips across the soft needles of the decorations lining the top. Could she allow herself to give Max a second chance?

Then she noticed a small burlap bag right in the middle of the desktop. A bright red ribbon tied it closed. Picking it up, Olivia undid the bow and peeked inside. The bag was full of orange jellies, her favorite. She clutched the bag to her chest. *Damn you, Max. You're not going to make it easy for me to say no, are you?*

Chapter Nineteen

"STILL HIDING, MA *chérie*?" Julien closed the library door behind him.

Olivia looked up from her book. "Julien, I'm not hiding. I am simply enjoying a good book by the fire."

Julien chuckled. "May I join you?"

"Of course." She motioned to the chair across from her. The sounds of muffled hammering filtered through the door. Olivia grimaced. "He has been at it all morning. When I walked past him earlier, he was standing precariously on a tall ladder tacking greenery to the molding above the front door. When I inquired why he hadn't asked Daniels to take care of it, he grinned and said the job needed a creative eye."

"The decoration looks quite nice in the main hall. When I passed him last, he and Louisa were wrapping the stair railing with garland."

"The dinner party was meant to be a simple affair. Unfortunately, I fear there is no such thing when it comes to Mrs. Drake and her family."

Julien shrugged. "It will be fun. All of your favorite people will be here, no? So, tell me, why are you hiding with your book?"

"I am not hiding. I'm just not in the mood for Christmas celebrations. Why must we make such a fuss?"

"I am happy to spend Christmas here with you and your guests. I always envied that Henry would return here in December and make merry for Christmastide. I told him I went to visit my family, but in truth, I spent the holiday alone."

"Oh, Julien. How awful to be alone at Christmas." Olivia leaned forward and laid her hand on his arm. "I don't mean to sound so grouchy. It's just that celebrating Christmas without Henry feels wrong. He was the arbitrator of fun. He loved Christmas. I miss him."

Julien took her hand in both of his. "I miss him, too." After a moment, he released her. "Are you sure it's not the new earl that has you hiding? His eyes watched you very carefully last night at dinner. He wears his feelings on his sleeve."

Olivia let out a sigh. She had felt his watchful gaze too. But she had been grateful Max hadn't tried to press her about his question from the bookstore. Julien leaned back with his hands folded together and waited patiently for her answer. Olivia bit her lower lip. "We kissed yesterday in the bookshop."

Julien's eyes widened. "Well, that explains all his staring. It does not explain why you are hiding from him. Was his kiss unwanted? Did he force his attentions on you?"

"No, nothing like that. It was unexpected...how I felt was unexpected." She shook her head. "It's complicated."

"Attraction is never complicated. Olivia, I know that you and Henry had a platonic arrangement. Did you not ever take a lover during the years you were married?"

She felt her cheeks heat, and she placed her hands on them. "No!"

"Whyever not? Henry had me; I know he wouldn't have minded."

Henry had said as much to her once. But the idea of taking a lover had seemed so blasé, so very not like her. She had never met anyone who had sparked her interest even. She had been content with her friendships, her estate, and the occasional trip to London to visit with her husband. Except now she had this terrible ache, this desire for that fire that had consumed her yesterday when Max's body had pressed against hers, his lips searing hers with his kisses.

"Chérie, it is obvious this man desires you. So let yourself be desired for once. I sense he will make a good lover." Julien chuckled. "He is a fine specimen of a man."

Olivia gaped open-mouthed at his comment. Julien's frankness shocked her. No one she knew spoke so openly about intimacy. It made her wonder, could she take a lover? Could she take Max as a lover?

The door flung open, and the fine specimen of a man filled the doorway. Max's gaze swung between her and Julien, and his brow wrinkled briefly. "Olivia, I could use your opinion about something. Will you come to take a look?"

She glanced at Julien, who just gave her a broad wink.

"He desires your opinion, Olivia. Go see what he needs."

Olivia sent him a quelling look before rising from her chair. "Of course, I'm happy to help."

Chapter Twenty

MAX WINGED OUT his elbow, and Olivia slid her hand through without hesitation, offering him a smile. The tightness in his chest loosened, and he tugged her close to his side. He swore she had been avoiding him since their kiss yesterday. The kiss had righted something in him. He wanted more kisses, more sighs of pleasure, more of Livvy. Max had a plan. He just needed to move slowly and let his actions show her how much he cared.

"Come see the drawing room. There is some discussion about the symmetry of the star. You must come be on my side."

"The star?" she asked.

"Yes, my mother and sister always weave the greenery into a star to hang over the fireplace. But Louisa insists it's crooked. I think it's fine; it's a five-pointed star; how can it be crooked?"

He guided them down the hallway toward the drawing room. At the top of the stairs, Olivia paused on the landing. She stepped over to the railing and Max joined her to look down onto the entrance hall. Greenery draped the front doors and wound up the staircase railing. Mr. Galey had hauled two small evergreens from the back terrace to flank the doorway, and Ginny had wrapped the dwarf trees in bright gold ribbon. Overall, he thought it looked quite festive. He leaned close to Olivia. "What do you think?"

"It's beautiful. And it smells divine in here."

She smelled divine. A light floral scent filled his nose and made him think of her laid out in a meadow of wildflowers. She would beckon for him to join her, and they would make love under the warm summer sun. Max sucked in a deep breath and stepped back from her intoxicating scent. Olivia turned to face him. He hoped his expression did not give away his lustful thoughts.

"Did you do this all yourself?" she asked.

He shook his head. "No, I enlisted the staff. It turns out they are quite efficient."

"It's because they do it every year." She gave a wry twist of her lips. "Except last year, of course."

He reached for her hand and ran his thumb across the soft skin. "Olivia—"

"No, it's all right. Yesterday after you left, I quite enjoyed the decorations in the shop. It didn't make me sad as I thought it would. On the contrary, they raised my spirits." She lifted her gaze to look at him through her lashes. "Thank you for the gift. They were delicious."

"You're welcome." He tugged her hand. "Let's go see the drawing room."

When they entered the drawing room, his sisters were still bickering about the ribbon choices. Ginny felt that gold ribbon should be the theme for the room, but Louisa preferred the red, citing it was more festive. "I have brought a neutral party to help make decisions," Max announced.

"Excellent!" Ginny held up a gold bow she'd made. "Olivia, don't you think this gold ribbon is divine?"

Olivia nodded. "It's very pretty."

Louisa rushed forward. "Don't you think that the red ribbon is more Christmas-y?" She held up a length of red velvet ribbon.

Realizing she had stepped into the middle of an argument, Olivia glanced at him. Max held his hands up. "I told them I did not have an opinion about the ribbon."

Olivia turned her attention back to his sisters. "Well, I think the red and gold complement each other nicely. Why not use them both? We could intertwine the two colors and make a pretty garland or attach the gold bows to the red ribbon and drape it along the top of the big mirror over there." She gestured across the room.

Ginny and Louisa both nodded. "Yes, you're right. That could work."

Max winked at Olivia. "Here, tell me is the star straight? Should one of the points be at the top?" They walked down to the other end of the room where the cavernous fireplace dominated the wall. The girls trailed after them.

"I think that the two points should be at the top. It's more aesthetically pleasing," Ginny said.

"I agree," Louisa said. "But Max is being unreasonable and refuses to change it."

Olivia stood for several moments in front of the fireplace. Max couldn't help smile at her serious expression as she contemplated the star. Finally, he gave her shoulder a gentle nudge with his. "Well, what's the verdict? You decide."

"I agree with Max. I like the star with the one point on top. It feels more symmetrical."

"Thank you." Max leaned over and kissed her cheek before turning to his sisters. "Ha. Go back to your ribbons."

Both girls folded their arms across their chests, expressions mulish. Olivia bit down on her bottom lip as she faced their disappointed expressions. But Max stood his ground, and his sisters turned away to go make their ribbon garland.

Olivia slid a glance his way, her expression apprehensive.

"Don't worry about them," he murmured. "They'll be fine." Max walked over to the window, hoping Olivia would follow. The garlands he had hung over each window had holly and rosemary and mistletoe in little bouquets tucked into the greenery. It was festive and sneaky of him, but he planned to steal as many kisses from Olivia's sweet lips as he could manage. With each kiss, he would convince her to give them a chance. Henry may have stolen her away, but he was gone and damned if Max wouldn't take this opportunity to win her heart back.

He stared out at the snowy landscape. Olivia came to stand next to him. "What are you looking at?"

"I've missed the winter. I didn't think I ever would, but I admit that I am charmed by the rolling fields covered in white. When we rode the property with Mr. Bromley, I couldn't help admire the beauty of this landscape."

"It is, in my opinion, one of the nicest pieces of land in Herefordshire. It's yours now to care for; its tenants yours as well."

He turned to face her. "I understand. I promise to be a good keeper of Belhaven."

Olivia studied at him for a moment. "I believe you will."

Her statement of faith buoyed him. He'd had plenty of doubts the past weeks whether he could step into Henry's shoes. Whether he had any business being the Earl of Rivenhall. Olivia gazed up at him, the velvety mink of her eyes tugged at his soul. If she believed in him, perhaps he could learn what he needed. Perhaps he could be the Earl of Rivenhall. He leaned down and kissed her. He kept it brief, aware his sisters were down at the other end of the room. Her lips were so soft as he brushed his mouth across hers, and even though he meant the kiss to be light, every inch of him craved more.

Olivia's eyes widened, and he chuckled at her startled expression. He pointed up. "Mistletoe. I couldn't resist."

She tipped her head up. Then a wry smile quirked up one side of her mouth. "I see that I will have to watch out for you this Christmastide."

Max shoved his hands into the pockets of his trousers and strove for an innocent expression. Luckily Olivia didn't seem mad.

"I will go help your sisters with the ribbon garland," she said.

Max watched her walk across the room, mesmerized by the gentle sway of her hips. He groaned under his breath. The rational part of his brain clanged a warning bell. *She has hurt you before; she loved another!* But when had he ever listened to that rational voice? Certainly not when he let his father convince him to join his underground business to sell stolen goods or when he had rushed into a fight in the marketplace to save a man he barely knew. No, he had made mistakes before and lived to tell the tale. He might get burned by Olivia, but what a way to die.

"It looks lovely in here." His mother bustled into the room. "Very festive. Oh, girls those bows are exquisite. What a nice job you have done." She untied her velvet bonnet and set it on a nearby table. "Max, I was looking for you." His mother crossed the room toward him.

"Hello, Mother. Did you need something?" He bussed her cheek.

"I've just come from visiting Lady Dearborn. We had a lovely chat over tea. Come sit with me."

He dutifully sat next to his mother on the settee.

"Lord Dearborn is quite influential in this county and well-loved for being a fair and a generous landlord. I think you could learn a great deal from him. They will be coming to dinner on Christmas Eve. I want you to make an effort to speak with him and gain his counsel."

Ah, Mother was already gaining the lay of the political ground. He nodded, sensing that his mother was just winding up to her actual point.

"They always go to town for the season. Their daughter is of marriageable age, and Lady Dearborn has been beside herself, trying to find her a good match. Apparently, she is quite a spirited *jeune fille*. Perhaps Lady Susanna would make a great candidate for you to consider for a wife."

A clatter came from across the room. Max saw Olivia bend over to retrieve a pair of scissors that had fallen to the floor. His mother called out, "Olivia dear, you are friends with Lady Susanna, correct?"

"Yes, she is part of my book club."

"Excellent. Will you make sure to introduce her to Max on Christmas Eve? I find that introductions are more meaningful when something personal for each party can be imparted. It gives them a common topic to begin their conversation. Don't you think so?"

"Mother, I don't—"

"No protests, please. You and Genevieve are each in need of a spouse. This is the year I will get you both appropriately married. And I don't want to hear any impertinence from either of you." She leaned over and patted his hand. "It's just an introduction. Don't worry; she is beautiful." At that, his mother rose and gathered her bonnet and gloves. "I'll see you all at dinner."

Once she had left the room, Louisa hooted with laughter. "Looks like you both are on the chopping block."

Ginny rolled her eyes. "At least she hasn't got someone lined up for me already."

Max strode across the room. "I have no intention of letting Mother choose a wife for me." He tried to catch Olivia's eye, but she was intently snipping a length of red ribbon. He rubbed the back of his neck. *Thank you, Mother.* Deciding retreat was the best strategy to avoid having this conversation in front of Olivia, he executed a small bow. "Please excuse me, ladies." Then he turned and exited the room. He had more mistletoe to hang.

Chapter Twenty-One

OLIVIA STARTLED AS an arm snaked around her waist from behind. "Happy Christmas," Max murmured in her ear, sending a shiver of awareness through her.

She twisted around. "Max, you scared the living daylights out of me!"

"Sorry." He leaned in to press his mouth softly against hers.

The slow caress of his lips was as intoxicating as a fine wine. She sighed when he pulled back. "Max, you have to stop kissing me whenever you want."

His hand still at her waist roamed up her back, spreading warmth as it trailed upward. "Why?"

"You know why." She frowned. "It's entirely inappropriate. Your mother is trying to match you with a wife, for goodness' sake."

"First of all, my mother can try all she wants, but I will be choosing my own wife. And second, if you want me to stop kissing you, you should stop standing under the mistletoe."

Olivia glanced up. Sure enough, above them was a ball of mistletoe hanging from a red ribbon. Good gracious, how many of these did he hang up? Max had kissed her under the mistletoe a half dozen times these past two days. Yesterday, when she met him to discuss this quarter's ledgers, he stole a smoldering kiss in front of the fireplace in the study. Later he kissed her in the library, then gave her another brief hard kiss just before she left to go to the bookshop in the doorway of the great hall.

Today, she had discussed the furniture arrangement for the party with Mrs. Peabody in the drawing room, and he had walked over and kissed her mid-sentence. Then he had the audacity to buss the housekeeper's cheek. He'd chuckled at the poor woman's shocked expression. "How could I resist two lovely ladies standing underneath the mistletoe?" Mrs. Peabody had twittered about the boldness of young men while she'd smiled and blushed.

"You are maniacal," Olivia retorted.

"Don't be cross." He pulled a box from behind his back. "I have a gift for you."

She eyed the pretty box. Her delight warred with her good sense. "But I haven't gotten you a gift."

"That's all right." He pushed the gift into her hands. "Open it."

Olivia glanced up at his face. Excitement shone like a halo around him. She tugged at the bow that secured the top, carefully unwinding the ribbon. Then she wiggled the lid off. Inside there was a nest of finely shredded paper. Her chest filled with anticipation as she wondered what could be hidden within.

"Good Lord, Livvy. What are you waiting for? Look inside." Max huffed.

"I like the anticipation. Once I open it, the surprise will be over." Olivia felt through the paper, and her hand closed around something smooth and round. She pulled it out and gasped. It was the pretty snow globe from the window of Mr. Ford's shop. She gently shook it and watched the snow swirl around the tiny ice-skating couple. "Oh Max, it's lovely, thank you."

"You're welcome. I don't think I will ever have the courage to get on the ice again, so you can just pretend this is us enjoying ourselves." He gave the globe a tap with one finger.

Olivia giggled. What was she going to do about him? She walked away and placed the snow globe on the mantel. Max's efforts to seduce her or charm her or whatever he was trying to do were working. Each kiss tempted her to take a chance. Henry's letter said he wished for her to take risks, but she wasn't sure she could forgive Max for his abandonment. Although one thing had been niggling her for days. In the bookstore, Max had said her statement that he hadn't written was false. What had he meant?

She ran one finger down over the glass of the snow globe. She and Max never skated elegantly across the ice like the miniature couple inside, but they had spent lots of time walking around the pond and across the fields in the summer months. That last summer day they'd spent together flitted into focus like remembering a hazy dream…

"Are you sure you won't come with me now?" Max said. "We can marry and live with my parents for a while."

Olivia flicked her eyes up to the upstairs window of the cottage where she knew her father was watching from behind the curtains. "He won't let me until you can provide for us. He made it clear."

Max gathered her into his arms. "I don't care what he thinks. Everything will be all right. I know it."

She raised a hand to his cheek. "He's forbidden it. Send for me once you've saved some money. I'll be waiting, I promise." She stood on tiptoe to kiss him, not caring what her father would say later. Blast the consequences. She needed to show Max how much she would miss him.

Max crushed his lips against hers with an urgency born of desperation and love. She ran her fingertips over his cheek and temple, kissing him back with all the love she had in her heart.

"Come on, you two. Are you not done saying goodbye?" Henry walked around the corner of the house. "We'll be late getting you off if we don't leave soon."

Max pulled back and growled at his cousin. Then he framed her face with his hands, his amber eyes full of soft emotion. He kissed her again tenderly, once, twice. "I'll miss you."

She gripped his wrists. "I'll miss you, too."

"By Jove, you two are so dramatic," Henry groused. "We'll all see each other soon. I'll escort her to Paris myself once you're settled. We've got to go."

Tears had spilled from the corners of her eyes. She couldn't hold them back. Max leaned in to brush his lips across her cheek, capturing the tears with a flick of his tongue. "Don't cry. I can't stand it when you cry."

She gave him a wobbly smile. "Then go. And I'll wait for your letters. I love you."

Max had pressed one last kiss to her lips and then walked away across the grass.

Henry gave her a salute with one hand. "Don't worry, love. I'll get him to the boat safely. I'll see you at Christmas break."

The drawing room door opened, and Max's family bustled into the room, interrupting her thoughts. Olivia pasted a smile on her face. Tonight was not the time to examine the past. Tonight, she had to tuck away her sadness and hurt and pretend to enjoy the party.

Marguerite immediately came over to greet them. "You look lovely, Olivia. Blue is certainly your color."

Olivia ran her hands down over the dark blue velvet of her skirts. "Thank you. Your dress is stunning."

"Thank you." Marguerite turned to her son and patted his cheek. "What a handsome Lord Rivenhall you make."

Olivia's heart ached at that. "Please excuse me," she murmured. She crossed to greet Max's grandmother. "Happy Christmas, Mrs. Stanley."

"Happy Christmas, dear. Come sit with me." Mrs. Stanley sat and arranged herself on the settee by the fire. Olivia sat obediently next to her. "I will tell you a secret. I do not enjoy this cold weather. I'd much prefer to be in the south of France."

"That's hardly a secret Grand-mère." Genevieve joined them. "You complain daily about the godforsaken snow."

"Belhaven Hall can be drafty in the winter," Olivia said. "I hope your room in the newer wing has been comfortable for you."

"Yes, dear. The room is very nice. But downstairs, I think I shall stay by the warmth of the fire." She patted Olivia's knee. "Doesn't my grandson look handsome tonight? He is such a good boy. Even with all that trouble his father got him embroiled in, he always kept a level head."

"Grand-mère," Genevieve muttered low. "Mother instructed us not to speak about Father's business. It's Christmas; let us focus on the future, yes?"

Olivia looked back and forth between the two women. Their expressions were mercurial as silent conversation flowed between them. What was the trouble Max had become embroiled in? What business? She glanced over at Max where he stood in low conversation with his mother. He did look handsome tonight in his evening clothes. His normal tousle of hair had been tamed back from his face, and his cravat was crisp and white against the black of his formal jacket.

The door opened again. Mr. Daniels entered. "Your guests have arrived."

Olivia stood and crossed to greet her friends. Max joined her as Charlotte and her family entered. Olivia leaned in to kiss her friend's cheek. "Welcome. Happy Christmas." She turned to Max. "You have met Lord and Lady Weston, and this is Lord Weston's aunt, Lady Diana Wells."

Max smiled at Charlotte and Daniel. "Welcome." Then he bowed over Lady Wells's extended hand. "It's a pleasure to meet you."

"And this is Lord Weston's brother, Lord Hawksridge," Olivia said.

"Welcome," Max said. His gaze swung back and forth between the two brothers.

Miles offered his hand. "To answer your unsaid question, yes, we are identical twins."

Max chuckled. "And I thought I was being discreet."

"We are used to it."

"I'll admit it can be confusing, even when you have known them their whole lives," Lady Wells said affectionately. "Charlotte is the only one who can reliably tell them apart."

"That's not true. I can always spot Hawksridge with his ramrod posture and polished shoes." A voice came through the doorway.

Everyone turned. Susanna and her parents crossed the hall toward them. She stopped next to Miles and gave him a broad wink.

Olivia ushered them into the room. "Lord and Lady Dearborn, may I introduce you to Lord Rivenhall. This is Lord and Lady Dearborn and their daughter, Lady Susanna Ashby."

"It's nice to meet you, Lord Rivenhall. I enjoyed visiting with your mother earlier this week," Lady Dearborn said.

Max bowed over each lady's hand. "It's a pleasure to meet you." He gestured to the room. "Please let me introduce you all to my family."

Everyone moved into the room, and more introductions were made. The room buzzed with good cheer. Lots of hugs were exchanged. Soon Eleanor and Lucius arrived with Sophia in tow. Lord and Lady Hornsby arrived next, and the last guests to come were Charlotte's parents. Lord and Lady Markham arrived with Charlotte and Lucius's eldest brother Edward and his wife, Katherine.

After introducing them to Max and his family, Olivia retreated to the other side of the room. She didn't care for her friend's family. If Charlotte hadn't insisted, she would never have extended an invitation to them. Lord and Lady Markham had disowned Charlotte after she broke her engagement with Hawksridge to marry Daniel, and they refused to hand over her dowry. Then, when Lucius spoke up on her behalf, they had also cut off his funds.

Even though Miles and Daniel had worked things out between them, Lady Markham had never recovered from the scandal and had not forgiven her daughter. Charlotte's older brother Edward had been the one to extend an olive branch to his younger siblings last summer in hopes of bringing the family back together. The Markhams could rot, in her opinion.

Susanna came to stand next to Olivia. "Poor things, I don't know who looks more uncomfortable, Charlotte, or Daniel and his brother. And that is saying something as

Miles never shows his discomfort, unless he is trying to lie, of course."

Olivia glanced across the room to where Hawksridge and the Westons stood. Charlotte placed a hand on her belly and straightened her shoulders. She murmured something to her husband and crossed the room toward her parents. Miles and Daniel stood with arms folded across their chests, wearing identical scowls.

"I can't believe she is going to speak with them. I purposefully placed the Markhams at the other end of the table from Charlotte just so she wouldn't have to," Olivia said.

"I think this pregnancy has affected her feelings about their estrangement. She doesn't want the baby to not know its grandparents."

"Even if those grandparents are awful?"

Susanna shrugged.

"Here, let's go introduce Lady Wells to Rivenhall's grandmother. She is a card; you will enjoy her as well."

DINNER WAS MORE fun than Max had expected. Olivia's friends were lively, and dinner conversation was full of stories and teasing banter. Max sipped his wine as the dessert course was served. He glanced down the long table to where Olivia sat at the opposite end. Mr. Galey seated at her right. The two were deep in conversation. Julien laid a hand on hers and laughed at something she said. Max's vision turned green around the edges. *Why was he always touching her?* You know why. You just don't want to admit it. A man and a woman cannot be so familiar without being intimate.

Max took in a calming breath. He was being unreasonable. He knew it. But damn it, besides the brief moments in the drawing room before the guests arrived, he hadn't a chance to talk with Olivia all evening. Not that his dinner companions were dull. Susanna Ashby was quite entertaining. And Lord and Lady Hornsby were an exuberant older couple full of gossip and good cheer.

"Lady Hornsby is famous around these parts for throwing extravagant parties. Two summers past, she had a fire-eater at her mid-summer fete. He could swallow fire and then blow it out from his mouth!" Susanna said.

"And he set the whole bloody dessert table on fire," Lord Hornsby exclaimed. "That man was a waste of my money."

"Dear, I told you, he was meant to dramatically set the rum pudding on fire, but the cook had doused it with too much alcohol, and the blaze was far bigger than it was supposed to be." Lady Hornsby laughed.

Max raised his eyebrows in surprise. "It certainly sounds dramatic."

"Well, I will admit I am always jealous of Belhaven's Twelfth Night parties. I was simply trying to create an experience for my guests. Now, Henry always went all out for Twelfth Night. One year they had all the characters from the song 'The Twelve Days of Christmas' here to entertain guests at the party. Everything from pipers piping to swans aswimming."

"Yes, I remember that one." Lady Markham spoke from mid-table. "One of those geese kept trying to eat the beads off the hem of my dress."

Olivia's lips curled up into a smile. "Yes, Henry wanted it to be as authentic as possible, even though I warned him that the birds would be trouble."

"Henry always had great enthusiasm for Christmastime," Lord Dearborn said. "Even if his ideas were over the top."

A sudden pang of regret pierced Max's heart. He hadn't ever gotten the chance to know the man that Henry had grown into. It was his fault. He could have been part of his cousin's life but had ignored his overtures of friendship the past eight years. With sadness thick in his throat, Max raised his glass. "To Henry, may we all live with the spirit of the season all year-round."

Lucius Grisham raised his glass. "To Henry." And the rest of the table followed with a chorus of "To Henry."

Max met Olivia's gaze down the long table. Her eyes shone with unshed tears, but her smile was genuine. She raised her glass to him before taking a sip. Max took a long swallow from his, trying to regain his composure. "Everyone, let's adjourn to the drawing room for games and music. My sister is excited to lead us on the pianoforte for the caroling." He stood and offered his hand to Susanna Ashby, effectively dismissing the usual tradition of hosting the men in an after-dinner brandy. He had no interest in it tonight, and it was his party after all.

Susanna's eyes widened, but she took his hand and rose. After a moment, everyone else rose and followed him and Lady Ashby out of the dining room.

Chapter Twenty-Two

"THAT WILL CERTAINLY cause a stir. My father lives for time away from the womenfolk." Susanna Ashby whispered as they walked up the stairs. "Not that I'm complaining, mind you. It's far more entertaining to be in mixed company."

Max shrugged. "I'm not in the mood for smoke and politics." It wasn't a lie. He intended tonight to be lighthearted and fun for Olivia. He had already ruined that by getting morose at the end of dinner. Time to get the *frivolity*, as Livvy called it, back on track. "Do you like to sing, Lady Ashby?"

"Oh no, I have no talent for it, but the Westons are both accomplished musicians. I have very few skills except for my horsemanship."

"Indeed? Tell me, do you hunt?" he asked politely.

"I do when the occasion calls for it. But what I enjoy most is training horses. This past spring, I went to see a show at Astley's Amphitheatre in London, and I have become obsessed with trick riding. I have been training with my two best mares to learn some tricks."

"Trick riding? Interesting. I have seen a Cossack regiment in Russia perform some impressive trick riding. It was a highlight from my trip to St. Petersburg."

"You have? You must tell me every single detail." She gripped his arm. "Perhaps we can plan an excursion, and you can tell me all about it."

Max nodded. Her forwardness typically would have put him off. He didn't want to be chased by young debutants looking for titled husbands. But he had a feeling the offer had little to do with her interest in him and more to do with her interest in hearing more about the Cossack riders.

Ginny took a seat at the pianoforte and began a lively rendition of "Here We Come A Wassailing." Guests filtered in and were offered wine and punch by efficient footmen. Max glanced around the room. Despite the change in protocol, everyone appeared in good spirits, conversing and singing along to the music. Lord Weston stood next to Ginny at the pianoforte and sang along in a deep baritone, his wife, seated nearby, joined in as well.

Farther down the room toward the large stone fireplace, another seating area welcomed guests to gather. The long wall to the right had three tall windows dressed with red and gold bunting. Lord Hawksridge stood alone by one, frowning into his glass of brandy.

Max leaned over. "Lord Hawksridge doesn't look like he is having any fun," he murmured to Lady Ashby.

"Oh pish, Hawksridge wouldn't know fun if it bit him," she said.

"Perhaps I should go talk—" Max began.

"Wait, stop right there." Lucius Grisham and his wife Eleanor were the last to enter the drawing room. He pulled her to a stop in the doorway. His wife gave him a quizzical look, but Mr. Grisham pointed up with a grin. "I simply cannot pass up an opportunity to kiss you under the mistletoe." Then he bent and kissed her with no small amount of heat.

"Newlyweds," Lady Ashby muttered from next to Max.

Max grinned. "I'm glad to see someone notice the mistletoe and make good use of it," he said as Mr. and Mrs. Grisham strolled up to join them.

"Beware," Ginny called out from the pianoforte. "He has it hung up all over the place."

"Has what hung up?" Lady Wells asked.

"Mistletoe," Grand-mère replied. "See, look over there. Lady Rivenhall, you and Mr. Galey appear to be standing right underneath another bouquet."

Max whipped around. Indeed, Olivia stood in front of the fireplace with Mr. Galey. Right where Max had kissed her earlier this evening. She and Julien both glanced up, and Olivia's cheeks pinked.

"Go on and kiss. It's tradition," Lady Dearborn trilled.

Mr. Galey laughed and slid an arm around Olivia's waist. He leaned to deliver a brief kiss causing the room to erupt in applause.

Max pursed his lips. "Excuse me for a moment," he said to Lady Ashby. She nodded and turned to her friends, and he wound his way toward the fireplace. Damn the man,

Julien's hand was still on her waist.

"Maxwell." His mother grabbed hold of his arm. "Just what do you think you are doing?"

He paused. What was he doing? Planning to heave her over his shoulder and stride away? Shove Julien Galey away from her like they were boys in the schoolyard? His inner beast growled in approval for both of those ideas, but his mother's hand squeezed his arm, bringing him back to his senses. He ran a hand through his hair. "Nothing, Mother. Just on my way to grab a glass of wine."

She raised one thin eyebrow. "Yes, well, let me help with that." She raised her hand, and a footman appeared with a tray of wineglasses at her elbow. "Dear, have you had the chance to talk with Lord Dearborn? I thought you might during after-dinner brandy in the dining room, but since you seemed so eager to keep close to Lady Ashby, I will not scold you for your decision to keep the company together. But let's go chat with the Dearborns, shall we?"

Max glanced over at Olivia who had moved from under the mistletoe to speak with Mrs. Kingsley and Lady Hornsby. He took a swallow of wine to settle his spike of jealousy. His mother gave him another sharp look. It was clear he did not have a choice, so he nodded and changed course to go speak with Lord Dearborn.

OLIVIA GLANCED AROUND the room with some satisfaction.

Everyone appeared to be having fun. She took a swallow of punch. Two tables had been set up at the far end of the room for card playing. Max played whist with his mother and Susanna's parents. At the other table, Mr. Galey played with Lord and Lady Hornsby and Lady Wells. Louisa had taken over for her sister at the pianoforte and was playing "God Rest Ye Merry, Gentlemen" with her grandmother nearby listening attentively.

A shout of laughter rang out. "Not even close!"

Olivia smiled. In front of the fireplace, a rousing game of blindman's bluff was in play. Susanna stood in the middle of the group with the blindfold on. Everyone scrambled their positions, and Lucius tapped her shoulder. She swiveled around to face him. She asked her first question. "Are you a gentleman or a lady?"

"A lady," Lucius answered in a ridiculous falsetto that made everyone laugh.

"A cheater, I see. Well, that helps narrow it down." Susanna reached out, and when her hands made contact with his chest, she harrumphed. Moving her hands, she patted the top of his shoulders. "Not tall enough to be Weston or Hawksridge."

Ellie giggled from nearby, and Lucius sent her a wink.

Susanna moved her hands to the top of his head. "Too-long, messy hair. It's Lucius!" Susanna lifted off the handkerchief covering her eyes. "I knew it," she exclaimed with a triumphant smile.

"Hey! It wasn't messy until you ran your hands all over

it." Lucius grumbled as he finger-combed through his mussed hair.

Everyone clapped loudly. It really had been an enjoyable evening. Max had been right; a little holiday cheer had done her heart good. There was still an ache when she thought about Henry missing all the fun. And the toast at dinner had almost brought her to tears, but happy tears. Julien had gripped her hand under the table, and she knew he felt the same.

She glanced down the room to where Max played cards and found his amber eyes trained on her. He had kept a close eye on her all evening. He smiled, and Olivia laid a hand on her chest as her heartbeat doubled. Oh, dear. Her fool heart had gone rogue and fallen in love with him despite the warnings from her head. Or maybe she was just realizing that she had never really stopped loving Max.

This was a disaster. How could she trust him with her heart again after he had been so careless, so callous before? Besides, how would it look if she opened herself up to a relationship with Max? It would confirm society's view that she was a social climber who would do anything to keep her position as Countess of Rivenhall, even seduce the new earl. The hateful gossip that had circulated when she and Henry had married was enough to last her a lifetime. And the main reason she preferred her local society over visiting town. She lowered her gaze and picked up her glass of punch. No, it would never work. She needed to start fresh away from Belhaven Hall. Redefine herself, perhaps as a bookshop owner. Yes, she liked that sound of that. She didn't need to put her battered heart through any more pain.

"Olivia, what a lovely party!" Ellie came to stand next to her. "I don't know when I last had so much fun."

"I'm glad. I was just thinking the same thing. Max's family insisted on the party, and at first, I didn't want to celebrate Christmas without Henry. But tonight was just what I needed to regain some of my Christmas spirit."

Ellie wrapped an arm around her waist and hugged her. "I'm so glad. Look at those two." She nodded her head to where Susanna and Miles stood in front of one of the windows nearby. "They are always bickering."

Olivia smiled. It was true. The two loved to exchange teasing barbs and often argued over silly things. She always chalked it up to Susanna and Miles both being very competitive souls. "You and Lucius used to be the same. Like an old married couple." She gently bumped her hip against her friend's hip.

Ellie's expression grew thoughtful. "Hmmmm," she murmured.

"Look who's gotten caught under the mistletoe!" Daniel hooted from the sofa, where he sat with an arm around Charlotte. "You're going to have to kiss her, Miles my boy."

Both Miles and Susanna's eyes went round as saucers. They looked up to find, sure enough, Max had tucked bouquets of mistletoe into the garland that draped each window. Susanna recovered first. She placed a hand on her hip and faced the room. "Hawksridge is far too prim and proper to play games or kiss under the mistletoe," she said with a laugh.

Miles's eyes narrowed, and in the next moment, his arm snaked around Susanna's waist pulling her toward him. He bent and pressed his lips to hers in a slow slide that lasted a few moments longer than was strictly necessary for a light-hearted kiss underneath the mistletoe. When they broke apart, everyone clapped loudly. Susanna turned and sketched a small curtsy, her smile in place. But Olivia didn't miss the high color of her cheeks or the way she avoided looking at Miles.

"Well then…" Ellie breathed out.

"My thoughts exactly," Olivia agreed.

Susanna came over and took the punch glass from Olivia's hand. Her friend drank the rest of what was in the glass and handed it back to her. "Come on you two, let's go play I Love My Love with an A." She strode back over to the seating area to join the others. Olivia exchanged a look with Ellie, who just shrugged. She slipped an arm through her friend's, and they went to join in the game.

Chapter Twenty-Three

MAX PULLED HIS gloves off and handed them and his hat to Mr. Daniels. "Mr. Daniels, I hope that the hot coffee is ready. I believe we are all frozen to the bone from the ride home from church."

"Yes, my lord. Breakfast is served in the morning room."

"Thank goodness. I know it is Christmas, but the sermon was needlessly lengthy." Max's mother handed her muff to a footman.

"When the weather is better, we should attend service in Marbury. Vicar Spencer's homilies are quite uplifting. He is Eleanor Grisham's father," Olivia said.

Grand-mère patted Olivia's arm. "Well, they did do a very nice prayer for your dear Henry's soul."

"Yes, it was quite nice."

Max noticed that Olivia hadn't taken off any of her outerwear.

"Let's have some food. I'm starving." Louisa started toward the back of the house.

As the rest of his family headed to breakfast, Max turned to Olivia. "Too cold to shed your coat?" he teased.

"Oh, no, I must turn right around. Mr. Daniels, can you

fetch the Boxing Day gift basket for the Johnsons and ask Mrs. Peabody to put into it a bottle of her famous tonic? Mrs. Johnson has caught the croup from their two youngest children. I expect it is because she has worn herself too thin this past month."

"Right away, my lady."

"You're going back out? But it's snowing," Max said.

"Only a little. Mr. Johnson approached me after church and said he could come by and pick up some of Mrs. Peabody's tonic for croup. When he told me his wife was ill, I sent him home and said I would deliver it myself."

"I'm coming with you."

Max had been up all night thinking about what may or may not be between Olivia and Mr. Galey and even more about Olivia and Henry. His anger at Henry for stealing away Olivia's heart still burned like hot embers, banked but not out. It mixed with his guilt to make a very bad cocktail in his gut. There were things to talk about.

"That's not necessary. I am perfectly capable of handling the small sleigh by myself."

"Livvy, I am coming with you. It has nothing to do with your capability with the damn horse," he growled. Then he strode away to find someone to fetch his coat. *Stubborn woman.* He wasn't letting her go out into bad weather by herself, no matter her protests. Why wouldn't she trust him?

When he returned to the front of the house with his coat, gloves, and beaver hat retrieved, she was gone. Had she left without him? Mr. Daniels came around the corner with a large wicker basket in his arms. No, she hadn't left without her gifts. He opened the door for the butler, and they walked out into the snow. The small sleigh with a fresh horse had been brought around to the front. Olivia was already tucked in under a blanket. A large umbrella opened above her blocked much of the snow from landing on her head. Max glanced up at the sky. The clouds were thick and gray, promising more foul weather. He pulled up the collar of his coat and slipped into the sleigh next to her. It was a tight fit, but perhaps their combined body heat under the blanket would help keep them warm. He was gratified to feel hot bricks at his feet.

Mr. Daniels passed him the basket, and he tucked it between their feet and then covered it with yet another blanket to keep the moisture off. He turned to Olivia. "Do you want to drive Miss Perfectly Capable? I can hold the umbrella."

Her eyes narrowed, but she nodded and passed him the umbrella. Then she took up the reins and they were off. "It's hardly snowing. There is nothing to worry about."

He wrapped an arm around her shoulders and scooted close. When she shot him a sharp look, he shrugged. "I need you to keep me warm. You know with my thin blood."

Olivia guffawed. Flicking the reins, she encouraged the horse to pick up speed, and they flew over the fields. The snow came at them sideways, the small flakes biting against his cheeks. The scenery went past in a bucolic slide of snow-covered fields and bare tree branches stretching out to the gray sky. Max thought again about Olivia and Julien Galey.

What was the nature of their relationship? He'd thought things were progressing well with his plans to woo Livvy, but if she and Julien were lovers, then perhaps he was just being foolish.

"Are you and Mr. Galey lovers?"

"Pardon?" Olivia twisted sideways to stare at him with wide, startled eyes.

"Are you and Mr. Galey lovers?"

"No! What would make you think so?" she replied.

"The way you act together, the way he always touches you. He is staying with you at Belhaven." Max raised an eyebrow in question.

"Julien came to Belhaven to mark the anniversary of Henry's death. We have a unique connection as the two people Henry loved most."

Max winced. He used to be in that category; someone Henry loved best. He withdrew his arm from around her and stared ahead. "But he kissed you last night."

Olivia poked him. "Under the mistletoe, which you hung all over the house. You have kissed me a half dozen times under said mistletoe."

"That's exactly what I mean. The mistletoe is just a pretense. I want to kiss you. I cannot stop myself from wanting to kiss you."

Olivia opened her mouth and closed it. "Julien Galey is a good friend, and he does not want more from me. We are not, nor ever have been, lovers."

They passed the pond where they had ice-skated. Olivia

guided the sleigh to turn left down a snow-covered lane.

Max snorted. "Oh, he wants more. Whether or not you know it." What man wouldn't?

She huffed out a breath. "No, he does not. I know this because Julien was Henry's lover, the love of his life."

Max's mouth fell open. He blinked several times as he stared at Olivia, trying to process her statement. Henry's lover? "Pardon me?" he croaked out.

Olivia brought the sleigh to a stop in front of a modest home with a thatched roof. She turned with a sigh. "Julien was Henry's lover. They were together for seven years." She climbed out of the sleigh.

Max scrambled out from his side. His mind still reeled from the news. He had so many questions. How had Olivia found out? How long had she known? Why hadn't Henry ever confided in him? They had once been as close as brothers. It hurt to realize Henry hadn't trusted him enough to tell him about something so important. Just one more hurt to heap upon so many others in the shattered remains of their friendship.

"Grab the basket. Let us deliver the tonic to the Johnsons." Olivia held up a hand palm facing out. "We can speak more after we get home."

Max grabbed the basket from the floor of the sleigh. Oh, they would definitely finish this conversation later.

Chapter Twenty-Four

"HAPPY CHRISTMAS. I hope that your family recovers quickly from their illness," Max said to Mr. Johnson as they readied themselves to go back out into the snow. They had spent a quarter hour chatting with Mr. Johnson and his eldest son. But the sound of the wind howling outside had steadily increased in volume, and when they looked out the window, they found that the light snowfall had thickened, and the wind had picked up, creating swirling snow dervishes.

"Thank you, my lord, Lady Rivenhall," Mr. Johnson said. "I'm sure Mrs. Peabody's tonic will help. My wife swears by it. Are you sure you don't want to wait out the storm? It looks to be getting bad out there."

Olivia shook her head as she pulled on her thick knit mittens. "No, I think it's best if we get home before it gets any worse. You need to take care of your family. We will just be in the way."

Johnson's son came through the front door and whipped his cap off to shake free the snow covering it. "I've brought your horse around from the barn and hitched him to the sleigh."

"Thank you, Will," Olivia said.

Max looked skeptically out the open doorway at the heavy snowfall. They were going to freeze getting home. "Let's go. This looks to get worse before it clears. Good day to you both."

They hurried down to the sleigh. Max tucked blankets around them and popped open the umbrella. Olivia snapped the reins, and the horse plodded forward against the wind. The umbrella proved to be useless, the wind snapping several spokes and turning it inside out within minutes. Max struggled to close the stupid thing. He took his scarf and wrapped it around the lower half of his face. Then turned and did the same with Olivia's scarf because her hands were tight on the reins.

"Thank you," she said, her voice muffled.

The poor horse struggled to pull the sleigh through the deepening snow. They had made it to the far side of the pond when the storm seemed to swell like a wave crashing against the cliffs. The wind whipped the snow around so fiercely Max could not see further than the horse's snow-covered tail. He heard the jingle of the harness and the whistle of the wind as it screamed across the pond.

"We have to get out of this storm," he yelled.

Olivia nodded. "I know. My father's house is not far. I think we can make it there."

Another quarter hour later, it seemed as though they had hardly made any progress at all. He had wrapped his arm around Olivia, and they were huddled together as the horse slogged through the snow. “Do you know where we are?” he said into her ear.

“I think so, yes, that’s the tree at the end of the drive. Just another hundred yards to the house.”

The house’s shadowy form finally came into view. Olivia guided the sleigh close to the front door. Max got out first and reached in to help Olivia out. “Do you think it’s open? Can we get inside?”

“A key is kept above the door on the molding. At least I hope it’s still there.” She shouted to be heard over the wind.

Max reached up and stuck his hand into the snow built up on the edge of the ornate doorjamb and felt around for the key. Just as he was about to give up hope, his fingers found the large metal key. He made quick work of unlocking the front door. Leaning close to Olivia’s ear, he said, “Go inside. I will get the horse into the barn. Open the back door. I’ll bring some wood in.”

Then he shoved her inside before she argued that she could help him. He stomped over to unhitch the horse—poor thing. Inside the barn, it wasn’t much warmer than outside, but it was dry and out of the wind. After a quick search, he found a brush and gave the beast a good rub down. “What a brave boy you were. What a strong boy,” he murmured. He covered its back with a wool blanket, and soon it was nosing its way to a pile of hay at the far end of the barn.

Taking a deep breath, Max plunged back out into the storm, making sure the barn door was secure. He plowed his way across to the kitchen door at the back of the house. Under the eaves, just as he remembered, was a woodshed. He gathered an armful of wood, dumped it by the back door, and then went back for two more. Finally, he opened the door and worked quickly to pile all the wood inside the kitchen. When he could finally shut the door, he leaned back against it with a sigh of relief. What an ordeal. He was fucking frozen to the bone.

Where was Olivia? He moved through the kitchen to the front room and found her standing in the middle of the space like a statue. No, statues didn't shiver. She had a flint box in her hands. He crossed quickly to wrap her in his arms. She leaned in against his shoulder, and he could feel her teeth chattering. "I t-tried to light the tinder b-but my hands won't work. T-t-too cold."

"You're probably soaked. Come and sit here. I'll get a fire going." He gently pushed her onto the settee and took the flint box from her frozen hands. Then he rushed to bring wood from the other room. They were out of the storm, but the house was far from warm. After piling the wood by the fireplace, he made quick work of starting a fire. As a blaze began to grow, he tugged off his gloves and hat and turned his attention back to Olivia. She still sat in the same position, shivering and chattering; her eyes stared blankly ahead. He knelt in front of her. "Livvy, where can I find blankets? Is there anything left, do you think?"

The house was sparsely furnished. A settee and two wingback chairs were set opposite of each other across the area rug. But no tables or desk graced the room. The bookshelves were bare. He did not even see a candlestick on the mantel.

"Livvy?" he asked again gently.

Her eyes focused on him, and he breathed a sigh of relief. "Maybe upstairs, t-trunks in the b-bedrooms."

He nodded. "Hang on. I'll be right back."

Upstairs, he did indeed find bed linens and wool blankets in a trunk at the end of a stripped-down bed. The walls in the room were painted a soft blue, and he wondered if this had been Olivia's room. Thankfully he also spotted two candles in brass holders sitting on the bedside table. He gathered everything and hurried back downstairs. The logs had caught, and the fire was roaring. But Olivia still sat frozen on the settee except for the chattering of her teeth. He needed to get her warm.

"Olivia, I need to strip you out of these wet clothes. All right?"

She nodded. He made quick work of her soaked gloves, hat, and cloak. Next, he knelt and removed her boots. Her wool stockings were wet through and he reached up and rolled them down and off. Her dress was wet as well in the front. "Stand up, please." She obeyed wordlessly, and he turned her like a rag doll to undo the buttons of her dress. It took him twice as long because his own frozen fingers didn't want to work properly.

Once he had her out of her dress, he assessed what else was damp. The hem of her petticoats were wet, but he didn't think it was worth taking them off just for that. Her chemise seemed dry enough as well. He wrapped a large blanket around her and led her closer to the fire. The heat from the fireplace seemed to snap her out of her daze. She blinked up at him. "W-what about you? You must get out of those clothes too."

He waggled his eyebrows. "I thought you would never ask."

Olivia laughed, but it was a weak sound. He dragged both wingback chairs close and set them to face the fireplace. He laid her dress across one along with the stockings and cloak. Then he stripped off his wet clothes, draping them across the other chair. Olivia watched with round eyes from beneath her blanket. Max stopped once he was down to his shirt and small clothes. He grabbed up the rest of the blankets from the settee. Arranging them into a nest of sorts on the floor in between the fireplace and chairs, he wrapped one around his shoulders and then sat with his back leaning against the upholstered chair.

"Come here, Livvy," he beckoned to her.

She moved to him and he settled her in between his legs with her back against his chest. Then he wrapped her blanket around the both of them. "Body heat should help."

She snuggled against him. "How are you so warm still?"

"Trust me, my extremities are frozen." He moved his bare foot against her leg, and she shrieked. He chuckled and wrapped his arms tightly around her. Even though it was midday, the storm still raging outside made the interior of the house dim at best. The fire crackled, and he stared into the flames. Slowly, Olivia stopped shivering. Her body turned lax in his arms, and he wondered if she was asleep. But when he glanced down at her face, she was also staring into the fire. Perhaps now, with her warm and snuggled against him he could ask his questions.

"Livvy?"

"Hmmm?"

"When did you find out about Henry and Mr. Galey? Was it after you were married?"

"It was before. When Henry asked me to marry him."

"I'm confused. Why would you marry him if you knew?"

Olivia sighed, and it sounded bone-deep. She didn't turn to face him but continued to stare into the fire. He didn't think she was going to reply, but then she began to talk.

"It all started here in this house. My father had wanted to marry me off to Baron Hadley. Hadley had seen me at a party at Charlotte's parents' house. He approached my father with the offer of marriage. My mother forbade my father from making the match. Baron Hadley was three times my age and had already buried two wives."

"About a year after you left, my mother got sick. The doctors said it was most likely cancer of the stomach. And when my mother died, my father wasted no time reaching out to Hadley to accept his offer. I stood up to him. I refused." Her voice cracked, and she shook her head. "I foolishly thought that would be enough. Surely he wouldn't force my hand. But I was wrong. He accepted Hadley's offer, and the wedding date was set for June. I was desperate. I didn't know what I was going to do."

"Why didn't you send for me? Why didn't you tell me what was happening?" Max ground out.

Olivia tilted her head up, her eyes filled with hurt. "I did. But I didn't hold out much hope. Your letters had stopped coming just months after you left." Her voice held a bitterness that sliced him. He didn't know why his letters had not reached her, but now wasn't the time to get into that. Her story was about Henry. So he waited for her to continue.

"The week before the wedding, my father and I fought. I refused to marry the baron; I said I would run away before marrying the old goat. My father became violent. He struck me, knocking me to the floor. That was when Henry came through the door. He was fresh home from university and received my letter. He was incensed by the scene he came upon and immediately took me out of the house. When I explained the whole sordid tale to him, he was quiet for a moment and then he said *marry me, Livvy.*"

Thank God for Henry. It was so like him to swoop in as the knight in shining armor. In his head, Max rearranged everything that he'd thought about Henry and Olivia. Everything he'd felt when he heard news of their marriage. Olivia in trouble, all alone trying to stand up against her father. Why hadn't she called for him? Frustration and anger expanded in his chest.

"Henry said he'd protect me. That marriage to him was far better than some moldy old baron. Then he admitted that he had fallen in love with a brilliant botanist, Julien Galey. His offer was of a marriage of convenience. Marriage to me would preserve his reputation and distract society's eyes from his relationship with Julien. In return, he would always take care of me and keep me safe. I never met Julien in person until after the accident. We immediately bonded over our mutual grief. He has been a good friend to me this past year."

Max couldn't sit still any longer. He rose from the floor and stepped to the fireplace laying his hands on the mantel; he absorbed the heat as his emotions churned. He should have been the one to save Livvy. She should have been his to love and cherish. He certainly wouldn't have offered merely a marriage of convenience. He whirled around. "Are you saying that you and Henry never…that the union was in name only?"

Olivia sat crossed-legged in the nest of blankets. Her chemise had slipped and exposed one creamy shoulder. Color stained her cheeks, and she lowered her eyes to her lap. "Yes, Henry and I had a platonic relationship. Our friendship was the basis of our marriage."

Max stood stock still, not trusting himself to respond without bungling the delicate trust she had offered by telling him the truth. Now was the time to offer some of his truth. He cleared his throat. "When I heard from my mother the news of your marriage, I was consumed with jealousy. I was enraged that Henry would betray our friendship and steal your heart away. I was so hurt that you would choose him over me."

Olivia's mouth fell open, her eyes round in surprise. "But you had moved on. I hadn't received any letters from you for almost a year. Not even when I wrote you about my mother's death."

Max went to his knees in front of her. He grasped her hands. "I never received any letters from you. I wrote you often the first year, and then I just gave up. That's the God's honest truth."

Olivia shook her head as if she could not wrap her mind around the new information.

"Will you at least believe that I would never have ignored your dire circumstances? That I would never have left you at your father's mercy?"

She traced her fingers down from his temple to his jaw. Her gaze piercing as she stared into his eyes. And then she nodded. Olivia leaned forward and kissed him. The press of her lips felt like absolution. He let out a soft moan. Her hands slid into his hair, and her kiss became more insistent. Max let himself bask in the glory of being kissed by Olivia. Her tongue slid into his mouth, and she sank against him as she explored. He wrapped a hand around her waist. Her lush curves fit against him from chest to hip, and nothing ever felt so right. She slowly kissed her way across his jawline, and he took a moment to take a much-needed breath. She overwhelmed his senses, his heart raced, and his cock hardened. "Olivia, perhaps we should finish our discussion. There are things I need to tell you."

She moved her lips to his ear. “No more talking. No more truths. Make love to me, Max. Show me what I have missed. Show me what passion feels like.”

Chapter Twenty-Five

OLIVIA SUCKED GENTLY on Max's earlobe, and he let out another low groan. The sound shot right down to her core. She clenched her thighs together. She didn't want to talk anymore. Too much to handle, too many things to process. All she could think about was her lost opportunity to be this man's wife. The years wasted. All those years spent alone in her bed, wondering what it would be like to have a husband in all the ways. To have not settled for safety and friendship but to be the center of someone's desire, of their world.

She rose to her knees and threw her arms around him, kissing him with every ounce of pent-up passion she possessed. She was no longer cold but instead was an inferno, ready to explode. The wind howled outside; the snow lashed against the windows. The storm mirrored her emotions. Max's arms tightened around her, and his mouth devoured hers. Hot and demanding, his lips angled, tasting and taking time to relearn the dips and planes. Their tongues clashed in a sensuous dance. She could think of nothing but Max.

She ran her hands over his back, tracing the muscles with frantic fingers. Frustrated with the fabric between her hands and his skin, she huffed. She broke their kiss and reached down to tug up the hem of his shirt. With a grin, Max slowly lifted his arms over his head. Olivia had to rise to her feet to lift the shirt all the way off. Her hands swept across the smooth skin of his shoulders, and she let out a hum of appreciation for the warm muscles. Max's hands were at her waist, untying her petticoats. He pushed one down, only to find another one underneath.

"How many petticoats are you wearing?" He growled.

"Three. In case you hadn't noticed, it's cold out there." She laughed aloud at his look of annoyance as he attacked the second set of ties. She continued to explore with her fingers across his shoulders and up along his arms, tracing every curve of muscle. The second petticoat hit the ground. Max made quick work of the third one, and Olivia stepped out of the pile of linens. Max scooped it all up and tossed it aside. He spun her around and divested her of her corset, which he also threw aside.

When she turned back, his gaze ran hot and hungry over her as she stood in her chemise. She blushed as she realized the thin lawn of her chemise was probably see-through in the firelight. His hands followed his gaze skimming up the outside of her thighs, over her hips and waist, and along the outside curve of her breasts in a tantalizing tease of what she really wanted from him, his hands hot against her skin.

She pushed him back onto his haunches and slid down to straddle his thighs. Max wrapped an arm around her waist and pulled her in for another searing kiss. Olivia couldn't hold back another moan as he notched her firmly against his erection. The hot hard length of him felt like a brand. She tilted her hips and rubbed her aching core against it in a slow slide. They both moaned, and Max's mouth moved to her throat. He leaned her backward kissing down her neck.

"My God, Livvy, you feel so good." He bucked his hips, and her mind went blank at the delicious sensations it brought forth. His mouth moved lower, blazing a wet path with his tongue to her breast. He dragged down the neckline of her chemise and claimed one puckered nipple. His hot mouth pulled at it eagerly and a sizzle of pleasure echoed between her legs. Her intimate muscles clenched in response, aching for him to ease this sharp need to have him fill her.

"I must be inside you. Livvy, Livvy…" He spoke desperate words as he moved his lips across her skin to the other breast, his tongue laving at the nipple through the material of her chemise. Then his hands grabbed the hem, and in one swift motion, he pulled it up and over her head.

When they were skin to skin, her mouth went back to his ear. "Yes, yes, I want that." She writhed against him.

Max gripped her around the waist, and twisting them, he laid her on the blankets. He shucked off his small clothes and was on top of her, one arm propping him up and one muscular thigh between her legs. His mouth was hot on hers; his other hand skimmed down her body, stopping to brush one finger along the soft skin above the curls of her mons. She quivered beneath him. "Max."

His fingers traced down her crease, and two fingers sank

into her. She gasped at the intrusion.

"Oh love, you're so wet. So wet for me," Max rasped. He gently drew back his fingers almost all the way before delving back inside.

Oliva writhed against his hand. She was wild with wanting, and he was playing with her, building her desire to a flashpoint. Then his thumb rubbed against her clit, circling it repeatedly as his fingers curled inside her. She couldn't take any more; her climax burst inside her in a river of sensations. She yelled out his name, her hips bucking as the pleasure of her orgasm pulsed and pulsed.

His lips against hers, Max murmured, "That's it, you come apart so beautifully. You are so beautiful." He shifted his hips, lining them up with hers, the hard length of him notched against her aching clit, causing her to gasp again. Then in one slow slide, Max pushed inside her. The stretch of his cock filled her just like she needed. He paused, frozen above her, staring down into her eyes as if he was waiting for permission to move. She wiggled her hips just a small bit, letting herself adjust to his size. Max continued to hold still. The tendons in his neck stood out from the effort. "Max, for goodness' sake…" She bucked her hips impatiently.

Max lowered his head and pressed his lips to her pulse. His hips pulled back and thrust forward again. Olivia tipped her head back, offering her throat, and Max bit down playfully. She wrapped her legs around him and abandoned herself to the pleasure of being claimed by this man. Each slide of him inside her ratcheted her pleasure higher and higher. His tongue laved at the spot he'd bit her and trailed back up to her ear. "Livvy, tell me you're mine. Tell me you'll always be mine."

His hips pumped against hers, the head of his cock hitting a spot inside her that made stars explode behind her eyes. "Yes, yes, I'm yours." Another orgasm ripped through her, and she lifted her hips as she pulsed around him.

Max gripped her hip with one hand and pulled out with a shout, her name on his lips. He threw back his head, and his seed pulsed out onto her stomach. His hips still thrusting as he orgasmed. She stared up at his naked body glistening with sweat and watched as he sucked in deep breaths of air. His lean chiseled torso was a sight to behold. She had trouble catching her own breath. Then Max leaned forward and caught himself on one forearm. His other hand gently swept errant hairs from her brow. His nose nuzzled hers. "Livvy, I—"

She cupped his face with her hands. "You what?"

"That was magnificent. You're magnificent." He kissed her hard but brief. Then he got to his knees and scooted over to his clothing on the chair. From the inside pocket of his jacket, he pulled a handkerchief. He returned to her and gently cleaned her stomach. "How do you feel?"

Olivia raised her arms above her head and stretched. She felt fabulous. More than fabulous, she felt satiated and relaxed and so very happy. She grinned up at Max. "Amazing is how I feel." She reached out and ran her fingers down the muscles of his stomach. He let out a sound that was half gasp, half giggle, which made her giggle. "Ticklish, darling?"

"Don't be ridiculous," Max scoffed.

She scooted up to a sitting position. Then reached out her fingers again, but this time Max caught her wrist. He yanked her against him, wrapping an arm firmly around her waist.

"Well, perhaps just a little bit." He nuzzled her neck, kissing her behind the ear.

The wind rattled the windows and a cold draft blew across her bare back, causing her to shiver as it hit her damp skin. Max frowned. He grabbed a quilt and draped it around her. Next, he got up and put two more logs on the fire, poking it with the iron to stoke the fire. Olivia laid down, facing its warmth. When Max returned to their nest, she lifted the blanket in invitation. He slid in next to her and pulled her close so her head rested in the crook of his shoulder.

She stared for a while at the dancing flames of the fire. The rise and fall of Max's chest under her hand slowed. When she tilted her head up to glance at his face, his eyes were closed. "Max," she whispered. His response was a soft "hmmm?" and a brief squeeze of his fingers on her arm. She brushed her fingertips across his chest, and he didn't even stir this time.

Olivia traced the smooth muscles of his chest and danced her fingertips over the grooves and dips of his abdomen, exploring until her fingers found a raised section. She lifted her head and peered down at a puckered pink scar about three inches in length on his left side just between two ribs. It was definitely new; she could still see the holes where the stitches had sutured the wound back together. What on earth? How had he come to get such a wound? Was this due to the trouble his grandmother had alluded to?

Her discovery was a stark reminder that she hardly knew the man next to her. The boy she had been in love with all those years ago had been carefree, funny, and a bit wild. But this Max had his own experiences and trials which had shaped who he was today. She ran a finger along the scar.

What was she doing? She had instigated their lovemaking. She had told him to show her what she'd been missing. *Dear Lord*, when had she become so brazen? It wasn't at all like her to take such a risk. She sat up and stared down at Max's handsome face, so relaxed in sleep. This was sure to be folly, and she the fool who let her passions lead her there.

Chapter Twenty-Six

SUN SLANTED INTO his eyes as he cracked them open. Max blinked several times, trying to wake up. He ran a hand down over his face and pushed himself to a seated position. The late afternoon sun shone outside. The storm had passed through. He was alone on the floor in the bed of blankets they had made love on. Where was Livvy? He twisted to scan the room and spotted her in front of one of the windows, her back to him, still wrapped head to foot in a quilt. Max rose and padded over to wrap his arms around her from behind. She stiffened in his arms.

"I see the storm has passed through," he said.

She nodded.

"How long did I sleep?"

"A couple of hours, maybe." She stepped out of the circle of his arms, and turned to face him. "Max, you're not wearing anything!"

"Neither are you." He slipped a hand under her quilt and stroked his hand down one smooth hip. She took another step back as though his touch had burned her. He frowned. "What's the matter, Livvy?"

"Nothing." She shook her head. "I think we should get

back home before it gets dark. Everyone will be worried about us." Her eyes flitted briefly to meet his gaze and then cast back down to the floor.

He took a step forward and cupped her cheek with one hand, forcing her chin up so she had to look at him. "Do you regret our lovemaking, Livvy?"

"No. Maybe…I don't know." The dark chocolate of her eyes swirled with regret, and it felt as though he had been stabbed again, this time through the heart.

There was a long moment of silence. Then her hand reached out, and she traced a finger over the scar on his left side. "How did you get this? It looks new," Olivia asked softly.

He dropped his hand from her face. The time for secrets was over. "I was stabbed by a knife."

She gasped; her eyes flew up to meet his. "Why?"

"The jobs I worked on with my father could become dangerous." He sighed. He never wanted her to know about his work as a fence, but he realized she would never trust him if she didn't know all of him. There wasn't a way to keep all of the last eight years a secret; his scar proved that. "That's what happens when you deal in stolen art. The characters you do business with don't always play fair." There, the awful truth, laid bare.

"I thought you went to Paris to work in a museum."

"I did. But after two years of toiling in the archives cataloging and filing, my father convinced me to step out of the basement and work for him. Apparently, working for the foreign service office did not offer the salary that would support my parents' extravagant lifestyle. He had been dealing in stolen art for two decades. After I found out about your marriage to Henry, I thought, why keep the respectable job? The museum job had been for our future, a future that at the time, I felt Henry had stolen from me." He shrugged. "After my father's death, I continued to run his business to support my family."

"But this September, I ran into some trouble." He touched his scar. "I almost died. But I asked God to spare me and promised that I would make a better life, a more respectable life for myself. The letter from Henry's solicitors finally reached me not two days later. Do you see? This is my fresh start." He ran the back of his knuckles gently down her cheek. "This could be a fresh start for us both."

She bit down on her lower lip. "People will talk. Everyone will think I seduced the new earl to keep my position and stay at Belhaven. There was so much gossip when Henry married me, a nobody with no pedigree. I'm not sure I can be the center of another storm of gossip."

"Do you really care what society thinks? I know I don't." He grasped her hands in a desperate grip. His temper built inside his chest. "You're what I want. You always should have been mine."

She turned her face away. "You *should* care. You are the Earl of Rivenhall now. Your reputation will affect your sisters' lives and prospects as well as your influence in the House of Lords." She sighed. "Max, we are not the same people we were when we loved one another long ago. And..." Her voice broke. "I don't know if my heart can risk any more heartache. No matter how tempting."

Every word she said was another small slice to his heart. She still couldn't trust him, even after what they had shared earlier. Old bitterness rose in his throat. "I think you are the same girl you always were. The same girl who was too scared to come with me to Paris when I asked. Too scared to take the chance for happiness, to trust that I could have taken care of you." All these wasted years, all the heartache. A draft raced over his bare skin, and he turned away from the woman breaking his heart all over again. "Get dressed. You're right, we should get home before dark."

Max tugged on his clothes with quick efficiency. He could hear the rustling of clothing from next to him as Olivia dressed. Then she was next to him, her eyes down, she clutched her corset. "Can you help with this and my dress, please?"

"Of course."

She placed the corset against her abdomen and presented her back to him. He laced her and then helped lift her dress over her head and buttoned up the back. Olivia's breath came out in jerky pants. "Did I do it too tightly?" he asked.

She shook her head and when she turned around her eyes were red-rimmed and watery. She reached out and placed a hand on his heart. "Max..."

He stepped away before he could be tempted to offer her comfort. "I'll go get the horse hitched up." Self-preservation propelled him toward the front door. The physical labor needed to shovel out the snow piled up in and around the sleigh helped burn off some of his foul temper.

The trip back to Belhaven Hall was silent, neither of them having anything left to say. As they drove up the circular drive in the front of Belhaven, the front door opened, and Daniels rushed down the stairs.

"Lord Rivenhall, Lady Rivenhall, you're unharmed. We were all so concerned."

Olivia took Daniels's hand and climbed out of the sleigh. "We managed to take shelter at the land steward's cottage. We got quite wet but nothing a good fire couldn't help with. I'm sorry we worried everyone."

"Both of us could use a hot bath. Lady Rivenhall first," Max said.

"Certainly, my lord. We will get the water boiling immediately."

They walked up the stairs and entered the main hall. Max began to shed his still damp outerwear. "Thank you, Mr. Daniels. Where is my family?"

"They are all in the drawing room playing cards."

Max nodded. "I will go tell them we arrived home safely. Please come get me when a bath is available." Then, without looking at Olivia, he strode away. He would inform his family they were fine, and then he planned to sink his frozen body into a hot bath and wallow for as long as it took to regain control over his wayward heart.

Chapter Twenty-Seven

OLIVIA SMOOTHED A hand over her hair and took a deep breath before going into the dining room for luncheon. She could do this. She could face Max and his anger. It was well deserved. But she was doing what was best for both of them. *Liar*, her heart whispered. She ignored it and pasted a smile on her face. When she entered, she found that her bravado was not necessary. Max was not there, but the rest of his family sat around the table.

"Lady Rivenhall, are you recovered from your ordeal? You still look a bit peaked."

"Yes, I'm better. Thank you. Yesterday was busy with handing out Boxing Day gifts at the open house, so I think I am yet a bit tired." That was an understatement.

Yesterday during the open house, she could hardly bear the undercurrent of hurt that radiated from Max as she stood next to him in the drawing room to greet their tenants. He hadn't spoken a word directly to her the whole afternoon. Mr. Bromley had participated in order to be introduced as the new land steward. He couldn't have made a better impression, and Olivia was surprised to find that she felt relieved to shed the responsibilities of running the estate. She was looking forward to getting back to her bookstore tomorrow.

It didn't help that the past two nights she'd slept fitfully. Tossing and turning, she berated herself for hurting Max. For ruining their beautiful afternoon together. But mostly, she had lain awake recalling every detail of their lovemaking on Christmas Day, every touch and moan of pleasure. Torturing herself with the sweet words which had spilled from him while he made love to her.

A dozen times had she wondered whether she had said the right things. Perhaps she should have kept her fears to herself and just enjoyed being Max's lover. But the fear of being hurt again was too large to be stuffed down inside. Everyone she'd loved had left her, Max, her mother, Henry. People leave, people die. She understood that was part of life, but it didn't mean she would open herself up to that pain again.

She reached for the teapot and poured herself a steaming cup. "Where is Max today?" she asked casually.

"He was invited to spend the day at Lord and Lady Dearborn's estate," Max's mother replied. "I think he and Lady Ashby hit it off on Christmas Eve."

Olivia's cup rattled as she set it down. She placed her shaking hands in her lap. "That's nice. Susanna is one of my dearest friends and a lovely person." She reached for a piece of bread and bit into it.

Mrs. Drake leaned forward. "Tell me, what is her situation with Lord Hawksridge? Is he courting her? We must assess the competition."

Olivia widened her eyes, hoping to convey sincerity. "No, Lord Hawksridge is only a good friend. Being Lord Weston's brother, he has become one of our group." All of that was true, but that kiss under the mistletoe had surprised everyone. No one would have guessed that Miles could be goaded into a public display of affection. Only Susanna could push him thus far.

Olivia filled her plate with ham and thick pieces of sourdough and baby potatoes covered in dried thyme and rosemary. She ate while Max's family chatted around her. Max was spending the day with Susanna? One day he is making love to her, and the next, he is courting Susanna Dearborn? *You pushed him away, you nitwit! He could be warming your bed, but no, you had to throw up your walls.* Olivia stuffed a potato into her mouth. Well, he didn't have to go running straight to another woman. She slathered butter on a piece of bread and took a huge bite.

"Hungry, dear?" Max's grandmother raised a manicured eyebrow. "I have never seen you eat with such gusto."

Olivia swallowed her mouthful of food. "Yes, everything is so delicious. But I think that's it for me then. If you'll excuse me, please." She rose and nodded at the table. "Perhaps I can join you all later for cards." It turned out that Max's mother and grandmother quite enjoyed spending their afternoons playing cards. They were always looking to rotate in new players for their running game of whist.

Olivia left the dining room and wandered down the corridor. As she passed the drawing room, she was drawn inside by the smell of pipe smoke. Sure enough, she found Julien reading the paper by the window, his pipe clenched between his teeth. He pulled it out and blew out a long stream of smoke. "Hello, chérie. Were you looking for me?"

She shook her head and wandered over to the window. The sun was out today, and the snow stretched out as far as the eye could see in a blanket of white over the fields. Her stomach churned as her imagination flipped through various scenarios. Max flirting with Susanna, offering her one of his charming smiles, the two of them laughing together, seated together on the sofa, their hands brushing, thighs touching.

"Olivia, what has you in such a mood?" Julien asked.

"I don't know what you mean." She folded her arms across her chest.

"You just grunted."

Had she? She lifted her eyes to the heavens. *Good Lord.* She needed to gather her composure. A ball of mistletoe and holly hung from a thin ribbon and it made her think of Max and his kisses. Reaching up, she snatched it from where it was loosely tied to the curtains. She turned to Julien; his eyes widened in surprise. She glared at him, daring him to question her.

Then she marched over to the next window and removed the ball of mistletoe there as well. Olivia stalked over to the fireplace. She had to get on her tiptoes to reach this one, but it came down from its nail with a satisfying rip of the ribbon. She dumped her armful of mistletoe into a basket next to the fireplace. Damn the man and his adorable traditions and charming gifts. Max would be turning all that charm toward a new target, but she'd be damned if she would leave him any excuses for kissing Susanna hanging around the house. Olivia grabbed the basket and moved purposefully to the door. "See you at dinner, Julien."

The next room to attack was the library. Then she had Daniels fetch a ladder and take down the mistletoe from above the front door. Finally, she made her way to the study. Max had kissed her here in front of the fireplace. *No more kissing boughs. They led to nothing but trouble.* She yanked down the mistletoe hanging above the mantel with a decisive pull. With the last one collected, Olivia let out a long breath. She set the basket down on the large mahogany desk.

This room already felt like it belonged to Max. There were piles of papers and ledgers covering the top of the desk. He had been hard at work learning how the estate worked. The pair of spectacles that he wore when he read lay atop a stack of books by one of the wingback chairs in front of the fireplace. The room even smelled like him, like coffee and cedar. She sucked in a deep breath. Was she making the right decision by pulling away?

She twisted around, and when she looked down onto the desk, she spied familiar loopy handwriting. A letter with Max's name scrawled on the front in Henry's unmistakable hand lay on the blotter. She flipped it over. The seal was unbroken. How very odd. Why hadn't Max read Henry's letter yet? *Oh, Henry, I believe you would be disappointed in me. You told me to take chances, but instead, I pulled away from him at the first moment of doubt.*

She set the letter down and reached for the stout gold clock from the desk, just a little after two in the afternoon. Perhaps she should have gone and opened the shop today. She certainly wasn't in the mood to play cards with Max's mother and listen to her wax on about him and Susanna. What was she going to do with herself the rest of the afternoon?

OLIVIA PACED BACK and forth across the plush carpet runner in front of her bed. Indecision ate at her. Nine o'clock. Max hadn't gotten back from the Dearborn's until nine o'clock. At Olivia's request, her maid had hurried upstairs to report the news the minute he arrived home. Had he really had so much fun with Susanna that he had spent the entire day with her? *Of course, he had, you ninny, Susanna is a delight. She is also your very best friend.*

Olivia crossed to her vanity and grabbed her brush. Running it through her hair in slow, steady motions usually calmed her and helped settle her mind for bed. She grimaced at her reflection in the mirror. Susanna doesn't even want to settle down and get married.

Why does this bother you so much? She had been stewing all day. She tried to read a book to distract her thoughts, but all her favorite books were love stories, none of which had happy endings. She had reread Henry's letter. *Travel, take chances, fall in love*, he had instructed. Her brush froze halfway down. She sighed and set it aside. *All right, Henry, I will take a chance. But if this goes all wrong, I'm going to spit on your grave.*

She glanced over at the clock, midnight. *Apropos.* Olivia rose, slipped her dressing gown over her night shift, slid her feet into her slippers, and grabbed a candle from the bedside table. She took a deep breath and exited the room.

Chapter Twenty-Eight

MAX SET HIS spectacles down on the table next to him and rubbed at his eyes. Reading by firelight wasn't making his mind tired, just his eyes. Despite the long day, he couldn't seem to shut off his thoughts. He had spent the evening at the pub in Marbury drinking Lucius Grisham's excellent ale and brooding. But the frigid ride home had sadly sobered the lovely haze the ale had provided.

Lady Ashby had been a surprise. He knew that she would be an entertaining hostess, but he had not counted on how sharp she was. They had a pleasant luncheon with her parents, and then she had insisted on giving him a tour of the stables to show him her horses. Along the way, she had peppered him with questions about his experience watching the Cossacks perform. A dozen questions later, she abruptly changed subjects and asked him quite directly what were his intentions toward Olivia. He'd been so taken aback that his mouth had hung open. To which she just laughed out loud.

"Maxwell Drake, you don't think I could see you mooning after her all during Christmas Eve? I know my parents would like me to like you, and you to like me, but I only invited you here to find out what your intentions are with my very good friend." She shot him a saucy grin. "And to hear about the Cossacks."

Something about her forthrightness had persuaded him to be honest. "I'm in love with her. I always have been."

Susanna's brown eyes widened at his statement. "What do you mean always?"

So he had told her the whole sordid tale. Not about Henry and Livvy's marriage of convenience, of course, but the rest. How he had proposed a fresh start, and she had rejected him. The words had tumbled out, and Susanna Ashby had been an excellent listener. Another surprise.

"She told us very little about you. Which means she must have feelings for you."

"That makes no sense," he replied.

"No, it does. Olivia is very private. The bigger her feelings, the more she shoves them down. It's like she thinks having strong emotions is inappropriate." Susanna's mouth tipped up on one side. "We are very different creatures, she and I. You have to understand that Olivia has dealt with a lot of loss in the past five years. You may need to be more patient with her."

Max stared into the fire as he pondered his conversation with Susanna. *Patience.* They had been apart for eight fucking years. He pinched the bridge of his nose. He wasn't sure he was capable of patience. A creaking sound came from across the room. His bedroom door opened, and a shadowy figure slipped inside. The door creaked shut, and Olivia pressed back against it. The candle she carried illuminated her beautiful face.

"Olivia? What are you doing here?" he asked.

"I don't want you to court her." Her voice rang out across the room.

"Livvy—"

"I know that I ruined our beautiful afternoon together. And that I said I wasn't sure...and that I hurt you...but you can't—"

"Livvy, come here," he commanded.

She blinked at him for a moment. But then she moved into the room and slowly came toward him with eyes filled with trepidation. His initial instinct to tease her about being jealous died on his lips. He held out a hand, cautious not to spook her. "Livvy, I don't care about Susanna Ashby. I care about you."

Olivia stopped in front of him. He reached for the candle holder in her hand and set it aside next to his book. Then he grasped her hand, sandwiching it between both of his. "I don't want anyone but you."

Her breath rushed out of her in one long sigh. "You don't?"

Words didn't seem to sink in with this ridiculous woman, so he tugged her onto his lap and kissed her instead. He sank into the kiss, gently sliding his lips against hers, sipping and savoring her unique taste. She sighed against his mouth, and he counted it as a victory. Olivia was thinking far too much, worrying far too much. Tonight, he would make it his mission to persuade her only to feel.

She wore naught but her nightclothes, and her hair was unbound falling in a waterfall around her shoulders. He slid one hand into her hair. It was just as soft and thick as he remembered. It had always cascaded down her back freely when they were young, and he had been quite obsessed with the golden locks.

Max wrapped his hand in a section of her hair, winding it around and around. Then he gave a tug to pull her head back and expose her throat. Her eyes widened in surprise, but a low hum of pleasure followed as his lips scorched a path across her soft skin. "I think you need to be reminded that you're mine. That we have always been meant to love one another." He nipped at the juncture of her throat and shoulder, not too hard but hard enough to get her attention. "Livvy, why did you come to my room tonight?"

Her eyelids fluttered closed. "Because I was jealous that you spent the whole day with Susanna."

He gave another tug on her hair. "And why were you jealous?"

Her eyes popped open. They flashed with heat. "Because you're mine."

He growled in satisfaction and crushed his lips against hers. Her hands slid into his hair, and she kissed him back with just as much desperation. He wanted to devour her. Taste every inch of her heavenly body. He let go of her hair to run his hands down over her curves. There was far too much clothing between them. He stood, taking them both to their feet. With a swift tug at the belt of her dressing gown, he had it off her shoulders in seconds.

Olivia's curious fingers were under his shirt and burning a path up over the muscles of his stomach. He sucked in a breath as she circled one of his nipples, scraping gently over it with her nail. In one swift move, he pulled his shirt over his head. Her hum of approval shot straight down to his cock. He unbuttoned his trousers and stepped out of them, never breaking eye contact with Livvy. Her hot gaze flitted down to his erection, and his cock pulsed in response. Her mouth formed a small *O* and she reached out and ran a finger down the length of him. When she went to pull her hand back, he grabbed it and wrapped it around his cock. "Don't shy away; satisfy your curiosity."

Her fingers gripped him firmly, sliding slowly from base to tip. Then her thumb swept over the head, spreading his precum around the tip. Her other hand cupped his bullocks, giving them a gentle squeeze. Max closed his eyes, his head falling back at the sheer pleasure of having her tender hands fondling him. Though he quickly reconsidered his comment, her curiosity might be the death of him. "Livvy," he ground out.

Her exploration immediately stopped. Her gaze flew up to his face. "Was that not right? Did I hurt you?"

He framed her face with his hands and stared into her eyes. The worry was back, the corners crinkled in concern that she had done something wrong. "God no, your hands on me feel amazing. Don't mistake my groans for anything but pleasure." Max bent and captured her mouth with his, plunging his tongue in to tangle with hers. "Let me show you what I mean."

He grabbed handfuls of her shift and began to slide it up over her thighs. When he got to her waist, she raised her hands above her head. But he didn't increase his pace, enjoying the slow reveal of each curve and dip of her body. Finally, he lifted the nightgown over her head and tossed it aside. He cupped her backside and lifted her off her feet, capturing her mouth again as she wrapped her legs around him. Then he walked over to the bed.

"No more worrying, no more thinking about the future or the past," he murmured against her lips. "Focus only on right now in this moment. Think only of my lips against yours, my hands against your skin, my moans of pleasure in your ears."

Olivia nodded frantically; her nails dug into his shoulders as she wiggled her hips against his erection. She was so slick with desire he almost lost control and sank into her wet heat right then. She let out a squeak of surprise when he tossed her down on the bed. "Oh, no, naughty girl. I have plans to ravish every inch of your delectable body. No rushing to the finish line."

The corners of her mouth tipped up into a wicked smile. She trailed her fingers from her throat down the valley of her breasts, across her the gentle rise of her belly, all the way to the dark curls below. "Are you sure? The finish line is so wet and aching for you."

Max almost choked on his tongue at her words. She

leaned back on her elbows, and the pose pushed her lush breasts out, her tawny nipples, hard as diamonds, begged for his lips. With a low growl, he grabbed her ankles and slid her closer to the edge. "Not until I taste your sweet quim and have you screaming my name." He sank to his knees.

He kissed the inside of one knee, spreading her legs wide. Taking his time, he placed open-mouthed kisses along the creamy skin of her thigh, working his way to her center. When he reached her mons, he wasted no time with teasing. He fell on her like a wild beast, licking up her seam, savoring her spicy tang on his tongue. Olivia bucked her hips and cried out. He laid a firm hand on her pelvis to hold her down while he feasted, tonguing her slick folds and flicking her tight bud. Olivia writhed, and her head snapped up. Her gaze ensnared his, wild and glazed with passion. Triumph raced through his veins. He gave her clit a long slow suck eliciting a scream from Olivia as she climaxed against his mouth.

The sharp scrape of her fingers on his scalp propelled him into motion. His throbbing cock would not be denied a moment more. He sprang to his feet and flipped Olivia over onto her stomach. Reaching for her hips, he thrust into her dripping wet quim. The words he'd spoken to Livvy earlier prophetic. All he could do was feel. Olivia's moans matched his own as he sank into her. Her hips pushed back against him at each thrust. He bent over her back and caressed her shoulder with his lips. "God, Livvy, I'm lost in you. You are everything."

Then he straightened and gripped her hips, and he allowed himself one last glorious slide into her slick heat before pulling out. His climax rolled through him like fire cleansing his soul as he pulsed his seed out onto the sheets. Olivia collapsed onto her stomach, and he crawled up the bed on shaky knees to wrap himself around her. She turned in his arms to face him, hooking one leg over his. Her smile was languid.

He pressed a kiss to her lips. "What are you thinking about?"

"You." Her hand smoothed over his hip.

He gave her another kiss. "Mission accomplished."

"Egotist." She gave his arse a light smack. "Don't distract me from my thoroughly satiated state, or I shall be annoyed with you again."

"Pardon? Why is it you were annoyed?"

She pressed her face into his neck and yawned, her warm breath rushing over his skin. "I can't remember," she mumbled.

Max rolled his eyes. He brushed his hand over her hair. "Sleep, my love." He kept stroking the silky waves until her breathing slowed, and it was clear she slept. Max grabbed hold of the edge of the counterpane and pulled it over them. She may wake in the morning with all her walls back in place. But he'd tumbled them for tonight, and he would scale them again even if it meant he had to flirt with every maiden in Marbury.

Chapter Twenty-Nine

OLIVIA SMOOTHED AN errant hair back into place before knocking on the door to the study. She hoped she hadn't upset Max by leaving him sleeping in the early morning hours. She hadn't wanted to be caught sneaking from his room by servants doing early morning chores. And truthfully, she had needed time to gather her feelings. Last night had been astounding. Max's possessive words had been thrilling and oh so dangerous. She wanted badly to be his, to let herself be claimed. But she knew that Max wanted more than for them to be lovers. He wanted, no demanded, her heart as well. The question was could she risk loving and losing once again?

"Come in."

She poked her head inside. Max sat behind the desk. He rose and gestured her over.

"I hope I'm not interrupting." She cautiously crossed the room, trying to decipher his expression. "I'm sorry for leaving so early this morning. I wanted to get back to my rooms before the servants were up. And you looked so peaceful sleeping." His hair curled damp against his collar, and his face was freshly shaven. She reached up to brush her fingers along his jaw.

"I expected you would run away." He gazed down at her. She hated the guarded look in his eyes.

She went onto her toes to brush her lips across his. "Can we go slowly? I feel as though I have tumbled over a waterfall. What's between us is exhilarating but also terrifying."

He arched one eyebrow. "Terrifying?" But then he smiled, and he kissed the tip of her nose. "We can take our time. I'm not going anywhere." He sat and pulled her into his lap. His lips nuzzled a spot just below her ear, and she hummed at the tingle of pleasure it evoked. "But I insist on kissing you whenever I want. I noticed all the mistletoe was gone and wasn't sure if I should take it personally."

Olivia frowned. "I may have been in a small pique yesterday at the thought of you kissing anyone else under the mistletoe."

"I believe I am quite enjoying your jealousy." He squeezed her hip. "Tell me more about how mad you are for me."

"Pffft," she sniffed. "And don't be kissing me in front of your mother. She still wishes you to court Susanna Dearborn. For now, let's keep our love affair to ourselves."

"I'm not promising anything." He captured her mouth with a brief scorching kiss that left her breathless when he pulled away.

Olivia cleared her throat. She darted her gaze around in an attempt to escape the heated determination in his. She spotted the letter from Henry peeking out from under the edge of a ledger. Reaching for it, she slid it out from underneath. "Why haven't you opened your letter from Henry?"

Max's expression shuttered, and he shrugged. It was her turn to give him a searching look. He lifted her off his lap to her feet, and she leaned against the edge of the desk. "Now who is running away?"

He sighed. "At first, I was still too angry with Henry. And now that I know the truth, I am afraid of what recriminations it might hold. Henry was my best friend, and I don't know if I am ready to hear what he has to say from beyond the grave."

"I don't believe it will hold recriminations. If anything, it may hold instructions for you about your inheritance. Henry was disappointed in your disappearance from our lives, but he loved you."

"Perhaps," he said noncommittally.

"I plan to open the shop this morning. Would you like to come to town with me?"

"Yes. I'd love to get a closer look at the items in the attic. My curiosity won't be satisfied until I know what's in those wooden boxes."

"Excellent." She leaned in close. "You know the shop still has its mistletoe in place."

Max smiled. "Let's go make use of it."

OLIVIA BUSIED HERSELF with a display of character cards for

Twelfth Night. The colorfully drawn cards each depicted a favorite character from beloved plays, especially the Harlequin. Hostesses would pass out a card to each partygoer to assign them a character for the evening.

She removed the travel books from the window and replaced them with the display of cards. Epiphany was only a week away. This year, Lord and Lady Dearborn were hosting a Twelfth Night party, and she was happy to relinquish her annual duties as hostess for the revelry and just be a guest.

The sound of boxes scraping across the floor came from the back of the shop. Olivia walked back and saw Max's feet on the steps to the attic. "How's it going up there?"

More of him appeared as he made his way carefully down the stairs, a large wooden crate in his arms. "You won't believe the contents of these boxes," he exclaimed.

Olivia followed him over to the table, where he set down the wooden crate. "More liquor?"

"Nope." Max lifted off the lid.

The box was full of lace and silk. Olivia reached out to finger the delicate French lace. "Mr. Buxley has crates of fine fabrics in his attic?"

"Five crates, to be exact. And not just fabric." He lifted out a piece of ivory silk and held it up. Olivia gasped. It was not a bolt of fabric but rather a finely stitched negligee. He dropped it back into the crate and chose another, this nightgown was in crimson silk, but the top of the bodice was a sheer black lace. *Goodness!*

She pulled several items from the crate and let out a little sigh of feminine appreciation at the silk fabrics. Then a nightgown in a deep blue caught her eye. She pulled it up and out of the crate. It was full length with a neckline trimmed in lace. The silk would fall over her curves to the floor. "This one is pretty and tasteful," she said.

"Are you sure about that?" Max took it from her and turned the negligee so she could see the back. She clapped a hand over her mouth. The entire back was a sheer organza. It would leave nothing to the imagination.

"Oh my!"

Max stepped close to her. "I can easily imagine your curves wrapped in blue silk as you model this for me."

Such a suggestion should scandalize her, but instead, she found herself intrigued. The smoldering heat in Max's eyes having no small part in that. Her breath hitched as she thought about how the silk would feel against her skin as his hands burned a path down her body. "I think you should purchase something like this for me, except in red," she murmured.

Max's eyes widened in surprise.

"Did you expect me to respond with maidenly protests? After all we shared last night?" She moved her lips to his ear. "No, I am quite drunk on the passion you have shown me. I want to explore, discover more. I am greedy for you."

Max's arms banded around her and his mouth descended on hers hot and demanding. She kissed him back with a desperation she didn't know could flare again so soon. If they were alone, she would be tearing off his clothes. Now that she knew what the contours of his muscles and how hot his skin felt like underneath, the layers of clothing were just a nuisance.

Max grabbed a handful of her skirts with a frustrated groan, and she wondered if he felt exactly the same. Then he nibbled along her bottom lip, and his tongue flicked out and licked the corner of her mouth. He pressed another hard kiss against her lips before pulling away. "This isn't the place to start this, no matter how tempting visions of you swathed in silk and lace are."

Olivia pouted.

"Later," Max said firmly. "Feel what you do to me with just a few kisses." He grabbed her hand and placed it against the impressive bulge in his trousers. "I doubt you want your customers to see me in such a state."

Olivia giggled like a schoolgirl at his pained expression. But she stepped away. "Yes, well, I have an engagement this afternoon at Charlotte's home. Diana has agreed to speak with us about her letters. So perhaps we can plan for a clandestine meeting this evening? I feel as though I will be quite tired and may have to get to bed early."

Max's eyes flared once again with desire, making the amber melt to molten honey. "Tonight," he promised.

Chapter Thirty

"THANK YOU, LADY Wells, for agreeing to speak with us about your letters," Olivia said.

Ensconced in Charlotte's library at Brooksdale, all her friends sat attentively around Daniel and Miles's aunt Diana.

Lady Wells looked around the circle. "I still don't know how my letters managed to find their way to you all after all these years. But when Charlotte explained how much they had meant to her, how they helped encourage her to take a risk when she met my Daniel, I knew it must be fate."

Ellie nodded her head. "The letters inspired me as well. In, well, a different sort of way when I was in London this summer with Lucius." She blushed.

A smile turned up one corner of Diana's mouth. "He had quite a way with words, didn't he?"

Everyone nodded.

"We would love to know the whole story. If it is not too painful to tell it," Sophia replied.

Diana sighed. "My affair with James happened a very long time ago. It still makes me sad, but it is no longer painful. I have learned that you must let go of the disappointments in life or else you turn bitter."

Olivia reached to her bag and pulled out the three letters they had recently found at the bookstore. She set them down on the low table in front of Diana. "These are yours."

Charlotte pulled a small stack of letters from the side table next to her and put hers on the table as well. "These were the ones we originally found last year."

Last, Ellie pulled five letters from her reticule. "These are the ones we found in the bookshop in London." She placed them with the others.

Diana stared down at the pile of letters. She chose one and unfolded it. A smile stretched across her face as she read the letter. "Goodness, I almost forgot how beautiful his words were." She looked around at them. "James was a talented writer. During his time as a solider he worked as a personal secretary for General Waverly. And later, the general asked him to write his memoir. It became quite popular among those who enjoy accounts of battles and heroism. Lady Tangredi had received a copy, and she hired James to write her memoir. You see, she led quite the colorful life as an opera singer, and she claimed she had been a spy during the first years of the war. Her husband adored her, and he supported her every whim."

"Fascinating," Susanna exclaimed softly.

"James came from a good family. His father was headmaster at Eton but passed away while James fought in France. His mother's sister married well, a baron of a small county in Dorset. The aunt was acquainted with my mother and how James and I became acquainted. Now, I will always remember the exact moment we met. It was at the Henderson's ball, my first season out. I was just returning from the dance floor, and his gaze ensnared me from across the room. His eyes were the clearest blue, like a summer sky. I glanced around, thinking he was staring at someone nearby, but then he began to cross the room toward me. He didn't weave around guests but rather strode right through groups and couples to reach me. He bowed and introduced himself. So scandalous, but it made my heart flutter at his boldness." She sighed and picked up another letter. This one made her blush. "I can see that you all have read that our relationship quickly moved to a full-on love affair. I took so many risks to be with this man. He was like a tornado of emotions, and you couldn't help but get sucked up into the whirl and power of them."

Olivia couldn't help but think about the whirl of emotions she felt every moment she was near Max. A mixture of exasperation, amusement, the ache of old hurt, confusion, and desire. She never could keep her wits firmly about her when he made it his mission to charm her. All the bitterness from the past melted away with every kiss of his lips. His single-minded pursuit to rekindle their relationship had left her no time to think or to reflect whether trusting him with her heart again might be the most foolish decision ever.

"What happened to split you apart?" Olivia asked. "Was it your family?"

Diana nodded. "My mother turned a blind eye to the letters. She was so focused on my older sister, Agatha, Daniel and Miles's mother. Agatha had caught the eye of the Marquess of Hawksridge. There was a whirlwind of activity that summer to get ready for their nuptials. Of course, it didn't help that Agatha and Hawksridge were madly in love. It only fueled my fantasies about how love could conquer all." She paused and took a sip of her tea.

"When my mother finally realized that the infatuation had moved past just letters, that I had compromised myself, she was frantic to cover up what she saw as a failure in her mothering. I tried to assure her that James was wonderful, that we would marry once he had some money saved. My mother wouldn't listen. All she knew was that he was a writer with no income, a man with no title. She forbade me from seeing him and immediately began her search for a suitable husband for me. She scheduled every moment of my time, hired a companion for when she could not watch me. I obeyed her for a few months, but his desperate letters kept arriving, and that's when I started hiding them all in the books. I was afraid that if my mother found them, she would destroy them."

"But he came to see you in London," Ellie said. "The letter described his jealousy over seeing you with other men."

"Yes, he came to London. I'd broken down and written him about my upcoming betrothal to Lord Wells. And I let him come to me at night. He literally climbed through my window, like some hero in a novel."

All of them nodded. Olivia sat forward in her chair, anxious to find out what happened next.

"James asked me to run away with him. He begged me to gather my things and leave that very night. But I refused. To run away meant to leave my family, my sister. My parents would surely disown me. James had no plan, no way for us to live. He promised he would figure it out if only I would trust him." Her hands twisted together in her lap. "In the end, he said he understood. He apologized for his rashness and left. But it had been one risk too many. A servant saw him climb from my window and told my father."

Ellie sat closest to Diana, and she laid her hand on the older woman's clasped hands. "We read his last letter where he broke it off. It was his last letter, wasn't it?"

Diana nodded. "I was devastated. But time and some measure of wisdom that comes with age have made me realize that I let the man I loved think that he was less than what I needed, that he wasn't enough. I let my fears dictate my decision. It was no wonder when faced with my father's anger; he gave up on us."

Everyone was silent as they absorbed the tale. Diana glanced around. "Ladies, don't look so morose. I married my George, he was a kind husband, and we grew quite fond of each other. But even that was short-lived. Life has many paths. All you can do is be open to what might be around the corner." She smiled, but the edges were tinged with sadness. Olivia wondered if asking her to talk about her past love had been selfish of them.

Susanna's forehead was wrinkled in thought. "Lady Wells, do you mind me asking, what was James's family name?"

"James Marlow, why?"

"Aha! I knew it. Once you mentioned he had gained some fame for writing Waverly's memoir, I thought it must be him. My father has read the memoir and has spoken about it at length at the dinner table. But ladies, we all know him from his other work, *The Siren of Skye*."

Olivia nodded enthusiastically. "Yes, I remember that one. We read it maybe three years ago. How could we not recognize the similarities in the prose?" She turned to Diana. "We often share books that we enjoy. It is the foundation of our book club. And we all enjoyed *The Siren of Skye* immensely. The author is James Marlow. Do you think it could be him?"

"Charlotte, do you still have a copy here in your library?" Susanna asked.

"Perhaps. It is all alphabetical by author. It would be there." She pointed to a shelf across the room. Susanna jumped up and hurried over to scan the books.

"You've read a book called *The Siren of Skye*? That is the name of the story James started the month we spent at the seaside with his aunt. He would read to me from his pages as he wrote. I made him promise no blood or war. He promised me a happy ending."

"Aha," Susanna exclaimed from across the room. She returned to the group. "I've found it." She handed the slim volume to Lady Wells.

Diana ran her finger across the gold embossed title. Then

opened the cover and flipped through the pages. Her gasp pierced the quiet.

Ellie leaned over to see what had caused the reaction. "To Diana, forever my muse," she read out loud.

Olivia swallowed a lump in her throat. Her eyes watered, and tears dampened her eyelashes. Dear Lord, the man had never stopped loving her. Luckily, when she glanced up, she was not the only one moved to tears. Charlotte, handkerchief already out, dabbed at her eyes. And Ellie sniffled, blinking rapidly.

Diana stared down at the page for several long moments. Then she rose to her feet. "Excuse me, ladies, I have some reading I would like to accomplish."

"Thank you so much for sharing your story with us, Aunt Diana," Charlotte said. "Don't forget your letters."

Diana scooped up the letters and clutched them and the book to her chest before exiting. Moments later, Daniel and Miles strode into the room. They glanced around, taking in all the sniffling noses and damp eyes.

"We've just passed Aunt Diana in the hall. There were tears running down her face. For goodness' sake, what's happened?" Daniel asked.

"He never stopped loving her," Olivia said.

Miles's brow furrowed. "He who?"

Susanna picked up an embroidered pillow from next to her and threw it at Miles's chest. "Get out of here, you two. Leave us be."

With identical expressions of surprise, both men quickly made their retreat.

Chapter Thirty-One

MAX LIFTED THE opener and sliced the seal on Henry's letter. Then he took a deep breath and unfolded it. He couldn't bring himself to read it, and he wandered over to the window. After a moment, he returned to his chair. The letter lay in his lap while he studied the fire in the grate. *Fuck it.* Max began to read.

> *If you are reading this, then you are Rivenhall, and I am dead and buried. Perhaps my maudlin mood these days is what has me thinking so much about death. But can you blame me? My father has died, your father has died, and you might as well have died for all the endless silence I have received in return from my letters. I genuinely mourn our friendship, you bloody bastard.*

Max ran a hand through his hair and stood. He paced to the fireplace. Henry's words were ripping his heart out. Then, with a sigh, he sat back down.

> *You are now the caretaker of Belhaven, for better or worse. If Daniels is still around, make sure he gets a proper pension when he is ready to retire, which might*

be never. His age is still a mystery to me. The same goes for Mrs. Peabody. Make sure to hire someone decent to be the land steward, as I know you have no earthly idea what you are doing. I've had to fire Mr. Wentforth for being a despicable bastard. Since then, Olivia has been handling the estate, quite capably, I might add. She is always full of surprises and is the best of friends, which I cannot say about you any longer.

Speaking of Olivia, this is my final directive for you. Stay away from her, you selfish bastard. You hurt her deeply with your damned silent treatment. I have had to pick up the pieces of her heart. I have had to protect her. I have provided a generous income for her future, so you just leave her be. You don't deserve her.

Henry

Max doubled over in pain. Henry's words felt like a punch in the gut. He tried to breathe through his nose. He was going to be sick. Besides his father, Henry's opinion was the one he valued most. *You don't deserve her.* It echoed in his head. Straightening, he walked over to the window. The snow-covered gardens slumbered. The weather was too cold to start any melting. Everything seemed frozen in time.

Yesterday Olivia came home from her friend's house in the early evening. She had crossed the drawing room and kissed him hello in front of his whole family. Everyone's mouths had dropped open, but Max didn't care one wit. He relished having Livvy's lips claiming his. Later that night, her lips had been on much more than just his lips. She had thoroughly seduced him, body and soul.

He crumpled Henry's letter and threw it into the fire. The devil with him. He didn't get to choose for her. Henry didn't know the whole of it. Max had fucking written her dozens of letters. Perhaps he should have come home and confronted her when he didn't hear back—realized that something had gone wrong. But dammit, at nineteen, he hadn't the maturity to think past his hurt feelings. And then, when he heard about their marriage, well, the anger at his cousin had consumed him. He knew it had been immature to throw away Henry's letters. Regret rose bitter in his throat.

A knock at the door interrupted his self-recriminations. He turned. Olivia stood in the doorway. "Are you all right? Your face is like a thundercloud."

Max battled to school his features into what he hoped was a welcoming expression. He held out a hand. "You are exactly what I needed to see. Come here and let me kiss you."

She moved across the room with a smile. He bent to kiss her, but at the last moment, he pulled her into his arms and buried his face in her hair. He sucked in a deep breath of her light floral scent. Her hand came up to brush her fingers against the nape of his neck. "Max, won't you tell me what's wrong?"

He shook his head. Then he took a step back and forced himself to smile. "I have news that I think you will be happy to hear. Yesterday, I had an idea about the contraband in the bookshop. I went to visit Mr. Buxley while you were at the Westons, and I asked him straight out about the origins of the brandy, paintings, and lingerie. As I suspected, he said that during the war he had been approached by local smugglers looking for a temporary place to store their goods en route to northern counties. They paid him upfront but never returned for their crates. He figured they had perhaps been killed. All these years, he has been too nervous about his part in the illegal activities to ever do anything about the crates. So, I told him that I could sell everything for him."

"You did what?"

"I have a contact in London that handles contraband goods. I have worked with him on several jobs in the past. I believe he will give me a fair price. I estimate that everything together could garner a nice sum, certainly enough to keep the bookshop open for quite a while. You're welcome." He spread his hands wide. Mr. Buxley had been quite cheered at the prospect.

Olivia paced away from him. When she turned back, her hands were on her hips, her mouth set in a thin line. "I wish you had spoken to me before just swooping in to save the day."

He was confused by her aggressive posture. "I thought you would be happy that the bookshop didn't have to close. You said it was important to the community."

She paced to the desk and turned to pace back. "I planned to offer Mr. Buxley for the shop. I was going to use part of my nest egg to buy him out so he could retire. So, the bookshop could be mine."

"But why would you need to own a bookshop?"

She raised her hands in the air. Her voice rose. "What else am I to do with myself? I need a purpose, a plan for my future."

"A plan for your future. I thought we had begun something new together..." Max's chest constricted. *You don't deserve her. She will never trust you after you deserted her.* He shook his head. "I can see now that you never intended to take a risk on us. You were planning your backup plan the entire time."

She shook her head wildly. "No. Max, that's not it at all."

But they both knew that was a lie. She had been running away from her feelings from the first time they had made love. He had done an excellent job at seducing her into his bed, but he'd done a damn clumsy job of stealing her heart.

She stepped closer; her hand reached out for his. "What I mean is that the two are not exclusive of each other. Max, we have only just begun to know each other again. You said yourself I cannot continue to live here with you. It is entirely improper. Your family expects you to be in town for the social season and see your sister out into society. I need to find a house in Marbury and some purpose in my life outside of Belhaven Hall. I was hoping the bookshop would be that purpose."

All he could hear over the pounding of his heart was that

she was leaving, that what he felt for her was entirely improper. What an idiot he was to believe that she loved him still. Romantic notions of her being his countess, of their children running through the gardens in the summers, and coming to ask him to tell them all about the ghosts of Hall faded like mist. He ran a hand through his hair. "Well, I've already promised Mr. Buxley the sale of his items. So, you will need to work out any agreement you want with him directly."

Max stepped back from her touch, and his gaze darted to the door. He needed to leave before he found himself on his knees, begging her to love him. "I need some fresh air. I leave in the morning for London."

"Do you have to take the contraband yourself? How long will you be gone?" Olivia asked.

"Yes, my contact won't deal with anyone but me. I'm not sure how long it will take to track him down." He strode to the door.

"Max." Her voice wavered as she called out.

He paused but didn't turn. There was nothing but silence from behind him. He closed his eyes briefly, then he reached for the door handle and left the room. He didn't stop until he crossed the hall and exited out into the freezing afternoon.

Chapter Thirty-Two

"LORD RIVENHALL," A voice called out from behind him.

Max stopped his descent of the front steps and turned back toward the house. Mr. Daniels stood in the open doorway.

"My lord, where are you going?"

Max's temper crackled at the man's imperious tone. "For a walk. I would think that was obvious."

"What is not obvious is why you would do so without donning a coat or hat. It is freezing. I must insist you allow me to dress you properly, my lord."

Max felt his cheeks blaze with heat. He cleared his throat. "Certainly." As the butler disappeared inside, he returned to the top step. In a few moments, the man was back. Mr. Daniels helped Max don his greatcoat and passed him his hat and a pair of fur-lined leather gloves. Then he plunked down a pair of boots in front of him.

Max began to protest that his shoes were fine, but Mr. Daniels raised one eyebrow as if to say *I dare you*. So, he toed off one shoe and stuck his foot into the boot. After donning the next one, he handed off his shoes. "Thank you, Mr.

Daniels." His lips turned up into a wry grin. "May I be excused now?"

"Have a good walk, my lord." Mr. Daniels bowed and went back inside.

Max just shook his head and strode across the lawn. The cold air was welcome as he tried to cool his temper. Henry could rot. Max kicked at a large drift of snow, flinging up a shower of white. But his guilt ate at him. Henry's unopened letters, the death of Henry's father, Olivia being coerced into marriage to a man she didn't want. And he had been halfway across the world, licking his wounds and nursing his anger. What a damn fool he'd been. He hunched his shoulders and headed to the east side of the property.

It took a good half hour to reach the memorial garden which housed the mausoleum that held all the Earls of Rivenhall. The black iron fence surrounding the area stood six feet tall, and the Rivenhall crest was affixed to the gate. Max pushed it open. He should have come to pay his respects weeks ago when he first arrived.

In front of him were two stone structures. An ancient stone building sat on the south corner covered in moss. The newer building was made from gleaming white marble designed in the Greek style, with columns standing sentry in front. Max hesitated to approach the building, his emotions still a tangle of guilt, grief, and anger. Instead, he sat on a stone bench under a large elm and stared across at Henry's last resting place.

"Fuck, Henry, I'm sorry I stayed away. I thought you

had stolen Olivia away from me. I was so angry." Regret clogged his throat. "But I won't stay away from her. I love her. I always have. And this is my opportunity to win her back. This is our new beginning."

He stood and paced, the frozen grass crunching under his boots. "She has experienced so much loss, and damn you for dying on her," he yelled into the empty garden. He turned on his heel and began to pace again. "And maybe you're right, and I don't deserve her, but it's not going to stop me from loving her the way she deserves to be loved." He paused and stared at the mausoleum. "She belongs with me, dammit!"

"I've always known the two of you were a pair. Even before you mustered the courage to kiss her that first time."

Max whirled around. A figure stood on the other side of the gate. A figure that looked just like Henry. Max blinked fast, trying to clear his vision of this apparition. Henry's ghost opened the gate and slowly moved inside the garden. He walked like a flesh-and-blood man. It looked like Henry, except the apparition sported a bushy beard and mustache that Henry never wore in real life. Max closed his eyes and took a deep breath. When he opened them, Henry stood close enough to touch, so he reached out a hand and poked a finger at his chest. Solid flesh.

"Max, it's me. I can explain."

Explain? He could explain? Henry was alive, which meant that Olivia was not a widow. Olivia's husband was still alive. His cousin was still alive. Which meant Max was not really Lord Rivenhall then. All his hopes for the future drained from him, along with his good sense. Max grasped the front of Henry's shirt, pulled back his arm, and punched his cousin in the face.

Henry stumbled back, his hand pressed to his right eye. "Fuck, Max. What was that for?"

"What was that for? What was that for? Why are you alive? Do you even fathom the pain you've caused?" Olivia's beautiful brown eyes filled with sadness as she explained why she didn't want to celebrate Christmas without Henry rose sharply in his mind, and he stalked forward ready to pummel his cousin into the ground.

Henry straightened. "It was the only way to free me to be with Julien."

Max stopped short. "So, you staged your own death?"

"Yes, the accident was staged."

"But the body..."

"A cadaver stolen from the hospital. They threw the carriage lamp inside to set the fire and make it impossible to identify the body, except for my family ring."

Max ran a hand down over his face as he tried to process. "A cadaver? You're a madman."

Henry strode forward and grasped the front of Max's coat. "I am a madman." His eyes were wild. "I faked my death so that I could be free to spend my life with the man I love. And then you don't show up for a whole fucking year."

"I didn't get a letter until September. I've been in Italy and before that in the Ottoman."

Henry sighed and let go of him. "Everything got bungled. It was just supposed to be for a few weeks. I left for France, assumed a pseudonym, and paid off one of the clerks at Knightsbridge and Co. to keep me abreast of when Rivenhall's heir arrived." Henry tugged on his too-long hair. "Julien was supposed to get his letter and be inspired to pursue his dream to get on the boat to South America. I planned to be on it and surprise him. I knew Olivia would be upset, but she is still young; she would be free to find true happiness with someone. This was to give us all a chance for happiness."

"Upset? She is devastated. They both are. You should know better than anyone that Livvy loves deeply." Max stared at Henry, taking in his long hair and beard, the rough brown wool trousers and jacket he wore. He looked nothing like his childhood best friend. But he was real, and he was alive. Max closed the distance between them and wrapped his cousin in a hug. "God, I'm so happy to see you alive, you fucking bastard."

Henry returned his hug before pulling back to grasp Max by the shoulders. "How is it you have gotten better looking as the years wear on? It's not fair to the rest of us."

"Damn it Henry, don't try to charm me. I'm so angry with you. How are you here haunting me in this damn garden?"

"I followed you from the house." Henry shrugged. "I've been looking for the opportunity to get you alone."

"The house? Aren't you afraid of being seen by someone?"

"I know every nook and cranny of the Hall, every secret passageway. It's not so hard to sneak around. Besides, I need to eat."

"What? Have you been living in the walls?"

"No, I arrived in England shortly before you. I have been hiding at the land steward's house. It's been empty for years. It's far enough from the village that no one ever passes by and sees the smoke from the chimney."

"Wait, were you there the day of the snowstorm?" Shit, had he been party to their tryst?

Henry shook his head. "No, I was at Belhaven, it was Christmas Day, and I just wanted to be close to him. I spent the afternoon hidden in the passage that goes from the library to the drawing room. Your family played cards all afternoon. Your sister is quite talented at the pianoforte. They sang carols and laughed. Julien looked happy. He never joined us for the holidays before."

Max pursed his lips. This was by far the strangest fucking conversation he had ever had. "Henry, why have you shown yourself now? Why me?"

"Max, I'm sorry about the letter. I wrote it a year ago, and I was still angry with you for deserting us. I wanted to hurt you." He stared off across the frozen landscape for a minute. "Olivia wasn't the only one that you left behind. Besides, that was before I found all the letters."

"What letters?"

"I found all the letters you sent Olivia and the ones she'd

written to you all together under a loose floorboard in the master bedroom at the cottage. I tripped over the edge of the board one morning. The bastard must have intercepted all the mail. He wanted her to marry that ancient baron, you know. He was going to force her," Henry growled.

Her father had intercepted their letters. Of course. *Goddamnit.* Max turned and walked to the edge of the garden. He gripped the bars of the fence and shook them taking out all his pent-up frustration and anger on the cold metal posts. Then he leaned his forehead against it. So much wasted time, so much unnecessary heartache.

"Max, I need you to bring Julien to me at the cottage. I need to see him and explain before he goes back to London. It's been too long to just surprise him on the fucking boat. He would throw me overboard now. Can you help me?"

Max watched a gaggle of geese waddle across the field. "You have to tell her, too." His throat felt raw with emotion.

"What? No. Why tell her? You said it yourself, this is your chance for a new beginning."

Max turned to face his cousin. "I can't keep a secret like this from her. You ask too much." He beat his fist against his chest. "I promise to bring Julien and her to the cottage tomorrow. But you have to promise to accept the consequences of your actions whatever the two of them decide."

"You'll give up being Rivenhall so easily? You'll go back to your life of crime? Oh yes, I know all about that. Do you really want to let your family down like that?" Henry's expression was defiant, but his eyes shone with fear.

Max voiced his own fear. "If he doesn't forgive you, what will you do? Come back from the dead, take back the mantle?"

"I don't know." Henry's voice cracked. "Do you think they will forgive me?"

Max put his hand on Henry's shoulder. "I guess we will find out tomorrow. I will bring them in the afternoon."

Chapter Thirty-Three

OLIVIA BANGED THE knocker on Sophia's cheerful yellow front door. She chewed her bottom lip as she waited.

Sophia answered the door moments later. "Olivia, what a surprise. Please come in."

"I'm sorry, it's unforgivably rude to show up at your door without notice." Olivia stepped inside the cozy house. The pretty two-story cottage was not too large for one woman but not too small if Sophia wanted to have guests come and stay. Not that Olivia had ever known her to have house guests.

"Nonsense. My door is always open for my friends. Come, I'll have Mrs. Kelly make us some tea."

Once they were settled in Sophia's pretty receiving room, Olivia leaned forward. "Sophia, I know that you never speak of your past. But I am struggling with something, and I wondered if I could ask you a question?"

Sophia raised her eyebrows. "I suppose so. What is it you would like to know?"

"Have you been happy as a widow? I mean, I have known you now for almost two years. Are you satisfied being on your own, or do you wish to have another husband?"

"Well, I would say I am satisfied being on my own. I do not wish to be under the thumb of a husband again." She sighed. "The reason I do not speak of my late husband is because he was quite controlling and cruel. I am happy to be rid of him. This time in England has been a balm to my soul. Time to do as I please, to read, make friends with whom I want." Sophia leaned forward. "You needn't be alone. There are opportunities for intimacy without commitment. Men are mercurial creatures that don't like to be tied down. It is just a matter of finding a discreet partner."

Heat rose in Olivia's cheeks. "But what if your partner wants more of you than you are willing to give?"

"Who are we speaking about? Let us be frank," Sophia asked.

There was a soft knock at the door, and Sophia's housekeeper Mrs. Kelly came in with the tea cart. Olivia was thankful to have a moment to collect her thoughts. She didn't even know really what she was asking, just that Sophia might be the only one of her friends who could understand her reluctance to let herself fall in love again. Charlotte and Ellie were happily in love with their husbands and sure to encourage her to give in and follow her heart.

"I am speaking about Maxwell Drake, my late husband's heir. You see, we have a history together. We were in love when we were young. But he left to Paris for a job, and well, things didn't work out."

"But now you have taken him as a lover?" Sophia asked.

"Yes." Olivia put her hands to her cheeks. "But at every turn, he wishes for more. He is so sure of his feelings for me, and it is very attractive but also scary. I told him about wanting to buy the bookstore from Mr. Buxley and have a house in here in town, and he seemed to take it as a personal affront. But what is wrong with me wanting to have something for myself that is separate from Belhaven? Something just in case?"

Sophia poured tea for them both. She took a sip of hers before replying. "Nothing, if the reason is that you wish to live independently. In fact, you are welcome to stay here with me and share in the expenses for as long as you need to find your own place. But this fear that you speak of, is it because you love this man, but you wish not to?"

Was it? Did she love Max? Had he slipped into her heart despite her well-constructed walls? Or had her love for him always been there like a daffodil bulb waiting dormant until spring? She nodded. "Yes, exactly that."

"I do not have any experience with love. My marriage was arranged, and there was no love in any part, only possession, only control. So perhaps I am the wrong person to give my opinion. But I do know that love is not an everyday occurrence. That it is something special, only you can decide whether it is worth the risk."

OLIVIA SPENT A pleasant afternoon at the bookshop. She

took pleasure in seeing customers come into read the paper or ask her for recommendations for gifts. She was learning that the stationary was the most popular item in the store. She would need to reorder soon. It may not be bustling with activity, like the tea shop next door, nor be essential as the butcher shop across the street, but she enjoyed the quiet of the place.

On her way home, she thought a lot about Sophia's wise words. There was nothing wrong with wanting her independence. She hadn't had many choices in her life. She always felt left behind, struggling to start over without the people she loved. Max had a new life to start as Rivenhall, he would be in London participating in politics, socializing, and bringing his sisters out into society. He would soon leave her behind again. But this time, she would be prepared. She would have her own plans. It was a sensible decision.

She snapped the reins, and the horses made the turn to Belhaven with smooth synchronistic motions. They were quickly becoming excellent carriage horses. The pretty mares high stepped through the snow, their matching black manes flowing in the wind. She pulled into the drive. Her tiger jumped down from his perch on the backbench and took the reins. "Thank you, Jimmy. Please tell Mr. Jackson that his hard work training these two is paying off beautifully. They are very well behaved these days."

"I will, milady." Jimmy hopped into the driver seat and led the sleigh across to the stables. Olivia started up the stairs, her thoughts still on Max. He would just have to understand her position. She would go find him before dinner and be honest about her intentions. She needn't involve her heart.

Chapter Thirty-Four

"GOOD EVENING, LORD Rivenhall."

Max swiveled around and the glass of brandy in his hand sloshed. Olivia stood in the doorway to the drawing room cool and elegant in a dark pink gown. He bowed and returned her formal greeting. "Good evening, Lady Rivenhall. You gave me a start."

"I can see that. What is the matter?"

"Nothing. Why?" He dropped his gaze to his drink.

She crossed the room toward him. "You pace when you are working out something in that head of yours."

Max drained his glass. "No, nothing to work out. Just having a drink before dinner." Lord, how was he to get through this evening? The urge to blurt out all that transpired today was strong. He walked over to the cabinet that held the liquor and poured himself another two fingers. He glanced over his shoulder at her. "Anything for you? A sherry?"

She nodded.

He poured her a glass and took a calming breath before returning to her side. She took a sip of her wine and tilted her head to look up at him. "This is the second time today I have come upon you in a strange mood. Are you sure there is nothing the matter?"

He shook his head.

"Because I wanted to speak to you about our conversation this morning."

This morning seemed like a hundred years ago. Everything had shifted, what he knew about the past, his future. "We don't have to. Everything is fine. We are fine." He leaned his elbow on the edge of the mantel in an attempt to appear relaxed.

"Max! You'll burn your jacket."

He jumped back. "Yes, of course. Let's sit down." He walked over and sat in a nearby chair. Embarrassed, he took another long swallow. The brandy burned down his throat. He probably shouldn't have poured this third glass, but if there was ever a time to have too much, the day you find out your cousin has returned from the dead is the day to do it.

Olivia perched on the seat opposite of him. A small furrow appeared between her eyes as she took a sip of her sherry. His thoughts clanged like church bells. Not a widow. Still married to his cousin. What would her reaction be when she saw that Henry was still alive? Would she be angry? *Of course, she would.* Would she go along with Henry's plan? Could she carry on with her life knowing that her husband was still alive? And where did that leave him? Leave them?

He glanced up and found her staring at him. He struggled to rein in his thoughts. "Um, I have decided not to go to London tomorrow. I think the sale can wait until the new year. After all, that contraband has been sitting in the attic for years."

"Oh, that's good. Perhaps it can wait until the roads are better," Olivia replied. The line of worry between her eyes eased. She gave him a soft smile. "I didn't want you to leave."

Max wished he could whisk her away upstairs and lock them away in his room for the foreseeable future. But that was impossible, tomorrow would come, and secrets would be spilled. Perhaps Henry was right, and they shouldn't tell Olivia. It was a terrible, selfish thought, taunting him like a little devil on his shoulder. Before it could sink its claws into him, he said, "I wondered if tomorrow perhaps you would come with me to your old cottage to take a final inventory of things needed to have the place ready for Mr. Bromley in the new year."

"Yes, can we do it in the morning so that I can still open the bookshop on time?"

"Certainly, what time?"

"Perhaps ten?"

"Fine." They would go over and surprise Henry. The bastard deserved it.

Olivia opened her mouth as if to say something, but the door opened, and Mr. Galey entered the room. "Good evening, Lord Rivenhall, ma chérie."

Good, just who he needed to see. Max rose to greet him. "Can I get you a drink?" he asked.

"A glass of wine would be nice, thank you." Mr. Galey

followed him over to the bar cabinet.

"Mr. Galey, Olivia and I will head over to the land steward's cottage tomorrow morning. Would you care to join us? It makes for a pretty ride." He passed Julien a glass of wine.

"I suppose so. I haven't ridden at all since it began snowing."

Max could tell the man was on the fence but did not want to be rude. "There is also something I wish to get your opinion on." Max improvised. "A tree that looks dead to me. And I wondered if I should have it cut down so that it does not fall onto the roof." Max sipped his brandy and waited to see if the man would take the bait.

"Cut it down?" Mr. Galey's eyes widened. "Don't be too hasty. Many trees dormant in the winter months may appear to be dead but will bloom again in the spring. I will take a look at it."

"Excellent." Max covered his mouth with his glass as a smile of satisfaction bloomed. Now, if he could just avoid making conversation with the two of them for the rest of the evening, he might stand a chance at keeping his secret until tomorrow. He would leave the dinner conversation to his chatty family. There was one definite benefit of being the only man in a houseful of women. Sometimes you just couldn't get a word in edgewise.

OLIVIA LAY IN bed staring up at the shadowy canopy. The

banked fire across from her cast a warm glow across the wooden floorboards. It was late, but she couldn't sleep. Max had acted so strangely tonight. He'd said everything was fine between them, but yet he'd been so jumpy and he hadn't said two words at dinner. She debated whether to go see him tonight. It seemed like a bad idea since she had firmly decided not to be in love with him.

She turned from her back to her side and fluffed her pillow before sinking into its feathery softness. How she wanted to touch him though, to be wrapped in his arms. All evening, this pull of desire pulsed in her veins. How was she ever going to live without him? Now that she knew the wicked way he aroused her with his drugging kisses, how good it felt to yield to his soft demands, to melt under his caresses. And the glorious way his golden skin stretched over taut muscles, the salty taste of it as she licked his throat, his chest, and along his rigid length. She flipped again to her back and dragged her nightshift up her thighs; she rubbed her clit as she thought about him.

The door creaked open, and Olivia bolted up. Max slid into the room. He closed the door behind him. "Livvy, may I come in?"

She reached out a hand to beckon him to the bed. *Thank God.* He crossed to the foot of the bed and, with a flick of his wrist, untied the belt of his banyan robe. He crawled up onto the covers, leaving the robe behind on the floor. "Livvy, I couldn't stay away. I need to have you in my arms tonight."

"I need you too. I can't think of anything else." She

reached for him, sliding her hand behind his neck to grip his hair. "How have you so thoroughly seduced me?"

He leaned in and kissed her softly. Brushing his lips against hers again and again. His hands cupped the sides of her face holding her in place for a barrage of tenderness for which she was not prepared. He kissed the tip of her nose and placed kisses at each temple. He nuzzled her neck right below her ear, and she could feel his intake of breath as he inhaled.

"You always smell divine, like a fruit tart fresh from the oven."

Olivia giggled. "My perfume is a mixture of florals with a touch of raspberry."

He nibbled at her earlobe. "Ah, that must be it. Raspberry tart is what you are." His mouth traced a path down to the crook of her neck, and he nibbled there as well as his hands roamed down to cup her breasts. His thumbs brushed against her nipples through her nightshift in a frustrating tease.

Olivia scrambled to her knees. She reached down and lifted her shift up and off in a desperate move to be skin to skin with him. But when she pressed herself flush against him, he unwrapped her arms from around his neck to slide her back a few inches.

"Oh no, you little tart, I want to go slow tonight. Didn't you say you wanted to go slow?" His hands returned to her breasts to play anew with her nipples.

Olivia moaned as he teased one tight nipple. "You know

that's not what I meant."

Max's hands stroked down her sides and over the flare of her hips. His fingers intertwined with hers as he gazed down into her eyes. "What if tonight was our last night? What if tomorrow could change everything? Would you let me love you tonight? Would you let me show you how much I love you?"

"What do you mean, our last night?" Olivia whispered.

But Max didn't answer. Instead, he dipped his head to capture her lips in a kiss. His hands continued to smooth over her skin. Teasing the dip in her back with his fingertips before skating them over her derriere. Then they traveled up her spine one vertebrae at a time before delving his fingers into her hair. All the while, he kissed her slowly, reverently. She savored every nip and brush of his lips, every thrust of his tongue as they melded together, breath mingling; he demanded her surrender. *Let me love you.* She was helpless to do anything but succumb.

She smoothed her hands across his chest, his heartbeat strong under her palms. Then he lay her down on the mattress, covering her body with his, and teased her with a slide of his rock-hard erection against her mound. She wiggled against him with a whimper. "Max." She scratched her frustration across his back with her nails. Finally, his hand slid between them, and he fingered her aching clit.

"You are so wet, darling. What were you doing before I came in? Did you have your fingers here?" He ran one finger along her seam and then inside her with a shallow thrust that wasn't nearly enough to satisfy.

She nodded her head frantically. Then she pressed kisses along the shell of his ear. "I was thinking about you, and I had to touch myself."

Max groaned, and the rumble in his chest vibrated against her. "You are a seductress, is what you are." He lifted her hips, and this time he didn't tease but instead thrust into her in a slow slide.

She gasped at the exquisite sensation of being stretched and filled by him. She arched back with a cry of his name. Max placed scorching open-mouthed kisses across the top of her breasts as he tormented her by stroking in and out slowly, rubbing her clit with each roll of his hips. He drugged her with his kisses, and his sweet words murmured against her ear. "Livvy, you are my treasure. My heart has always belonged to you."

She ran her hands through his hair over and over. Her body consumed by the pleasure of his sweet seduction. Her orgasm built and built to a frantic roar.

"That's it, my sweet girl, come apart for me," he murmured against her lips.

Helpless to deny him, Olivia's orgasm burst forth in a million bright pieces. Max pulled out of her with a roar as his release rolled through him, and he came across her stomach. He leaned his forehead against hers, and chest heaving, they both tried to catch their breath.

"Olivia—"

She put one finger across his lips. "Please, my heart can't

take any more. For now, can you just hold me?"

He nodded and kissed the tip of her nose. Then he climbed off the bed to cross to the washbasin. When he returned, he used a damp cloth to clean off her stomach. Tossing it aside, he finally slid back in next to her and gathered her in his arms. With a tug of the covers, they were wrapped cozily together. She pressed her face into his chest, breathing in the smell of sweat and sex. She sighed. So much for rational decisions involving her heart.

Chapter Thirty-Five

MAX STARED DOWN at Olivia's face in the soft early morning light. He studied the slope of her nose and the soft flutter of her dark eyelashes. He ran a featherlight touch of his finger along her delicate jaw. Today would be hard for her. He wished he could save her from the pain and what would surely be anger. But he had decided it would be selfish to keep Henry's secret from her. She deserved to know. No matter what that meant for their future. That is if he could convince her that they should have one. He rolled out of bed, trying not to jostle her awake. He needed more time, more nights of passion, more days of flirting and conversation and kissing. He would even take her ice-skating again. *Damn it, Henry, a whole year in hiding, and now you want to reach out to your lover?*

Poor Julien. Max pulled on his robe. No, he wouldn't feel sorry for Julien. He was going to be reunited with his love. Once he stopped being angry, he would get to spend a lifetime with the man he thought was dead. Max took one last look at the sleeping Olivia. She moved onto her side and pulled the pillow he'd been laying on to her chest. Max smiled. *Until later, my love.* Then he slipped out the door.

BY TEN O'CLOCK in the morning, the three of them were mounted on their horses and ready to ride out of the warm stables into the crisp, bright morning. Max turned to Olivia and Julien. "Ready?"

They both nodded. Olivia looked pretty as a picture in her forest-green riding habit and matching box hat. A tall pheasant feather waved cheerily as she rode ahead of him out of the barn. He again felt guilty that he was leading them to such a rude shock this morning. He sucked in a deep breath of fresh air and tried to enjoy the beautiful surroundings as they rode. The rolling farmland that surrounded Belhaven Hall would be green in just a few months. In the spring, the sheep would be grazing, and the fields would be covered in bluebells. They made it to the road and headed east down the lane. They had made the right decision by riding instead of taking the carriage. This mixture of melting snow and sucking mud would have been hell for the wooden wheels to roll over. Max guided his horse around a dangerous rut.

They arrived at the cottage and pulled to a stop in front of the barn. Max helped Olivia down. He gave into impulse and bent to give her a swift kiss. She raised a hand to his cheek with a smile, and they walked the horses inside the barn to let them munch on hay. As they walked out, Julien glanced around the garden. "Where is this tree you spoke of?"

"Oh, let's go inside first. We can look at it after we assess the house." Max strode ahead to the front door. He lifted the latch and entered the cottage. In an attempt to make as much noise as possible, he stomped the snow off his boots. Then he coughed loudly.

The other two came in behind him, and Julien shut the door against the cold. Olivia sniffed the air. "Why does it smell like there is a fire burning?" She hurried into the front room. Max gestured to Julien to follow her.

Henry stood next to the fireplace. He tugged on the lapels of his jacket and smoothed back his hair.

"*Henry?*" Olivia's voice rang out in the empty room.

"Yes, it's me." Henry moved forward. "I can explain."

Julien stood frozen next to Max, his mouth agape. Then his nostrils flared, and his hands clenched into fists. He strode across the room and shoved Henry squarely in the chest. Then he hit him on the shoulder and kept hitting against his chest repeatedly.

Henry stumbled backward. Holding up his hands, he pleaded, "Julien, please let me explain."

But Julien was beyond reason. He kept shoving at Henry. Max stepped forward to intervene, but then Julien grabbed hold of the lapels of Henry's jacket and, with one last push, pinned him up against the far wall. He kissed Henry, hard and desperate. Henry gripped Julien's face, and the two kissed like the only way to breathe was to be coupled mouth to mouth.

Then, abruptly Julien tore his lips from Henry's. He

stepped back and slapped Henry across the face before crossing the room. He flung himself into a chair, leaned forward, and buried his face in his hands.

Henry rushed over and went to his knees in front of him. "Julien, I did this for us. It wasn't supposed to be this long."

Olivia made a strangled sound pulling Max's attention from the two men, and he turned to her. Olivia had her hand on her throat. Her eyes were wide and glazed in shock. "Henry?" She swayed on her feet. Max reached for her. Her eyelids fluttered, and she fainted into his arms.

OLIVIA CAME TO with a start. Max's arms surrounded her, and he brushed his fingers across her cheek. She blinked a couple of times, trying to process what happened. They were on the floor. Max held her in his lap.

"You fainted, darling," Max said. He looked up. "She's all right."

Olivia glanced up and found Henry's familiar face looking down at her. "Henry," she croaked. How can this be? She reached out a hand, and her fingers were soon wrapped in a warm, solid clasp as Henry squeezed her hand gently. She looked back at Max. "Is this real?"

He nodded. "He appeared in front of me yesterday in the memorial garden like a bloody apparition. He wanted me to bring Julien to him, but I insisted you must know, too."

Olivia scrambled to rise. "You knew he was alive?"

"Just for the past twenty-four hours." Max helped her to her feet. "I'll let him tell you both the whole of it."

She swiveled around to face Henry. Alive. She couldn't understand. They had buried his body in the family crypt. He looked the same. Well, perhaps thinner, and that bushy beard covered his handsome features. But whole and unharmed. "Why are you alive? Dear God, Henry, what is going on?"

Henry pushed both hands through his hair. He took in a deep breath, his chest rising and falling. He turned to Julien, who had raised his head to stare at them. His eyes were gleaming with unshed tears. Olivia crossed to him and reached for Julien's hand. Suddenly she was so angry. It flared like fire in her chest. She turned to her husband. "Henry, you owe us an explanation."

"I faked the carriage accident. I hired two men out of Portsmouth to help me. One posed as my coachman, and the other waited for us a mile or so from the house with fresh horses. I left the Dunhurst's home early, begging off with a headache. Once we were out on the heath, I got out, and the two men handled everything. They cut the horses loose, put the cadaver they'd procured into the carriage, then set the whole thing on fire with the carriage lamp."

Olivia's mouth dropped open. "But why?"

"It was the only way I could think of to be free to be with Julien, to free us all. It was never supposed to take a year for Max to arrive and accept the title. I thought a few weeks at most. Then you both would get your letters. I hoped Julien would be inspired to take his trip. I planned to be on the boat and reveal myself there." His gaze searched out Julien's.

Julien opened and closed his mouth several times. "You ridiculous fool."

"And what about me?" Olivia asked. "You were going to let believe you were dead?"

"Don't you see darling, this way you could move on and find love. Our arrangement was never fair to you."

She shook her head in disbelief. She didn't believe for a moment that Henry had done this for her. He was crazy to have gone to such lengths to run away with Julien. "Where have you been?"

"France. Staying in a small village on the coast. Waiting for word that my heir had been found and come to take possession of the entail. Dying each day that we were apart." His eyes never left Julien. "I don't want to be Rivenhall anymore. I don't want to pretend we are just good mates. All I want is to disappear somewhere we can be together and never worry about what society thinks. Do you think the jungles of South America will be far enough?"

Olivia searched for Max. He stood alone by the window, gazing out. Did he feel like a pawn in this whole scheme of Henry's? As if he could feel her gaze on the back of his neck, Max turned. Their eyes locked. All she wanted was his arms wrapped around her. Nothing made sense. Her whole world was turned upside down. The only thing she was sure of was Max. She stumbled toward him. He strode across the room and folded her into his embrace. He stroked her back as she clung to him.

A few minutes later, Henry's voice came from behind her. "These are for the both of you."

Olivia twisted in Max's arms. Henry held out a long narrow box full of letters. "I have been hiding here the past few weeks. One morning, I stubbed my toe on a loose floorboard in the bedroom and found these tucked beneath it. Your father was intercepting your post."

Olivia reached out and picked up a letter from the box. It was addressed to her in Max's tight, precise handwriting. She stepped forward and rifled through the letters; there were dozens, some for her and some that had been meant for Max. *Oh, God.* Her father had kept them all. Hidden them. Taken not just the letters but their future. All those years stolen from them. Her breath shuddered in as a stabbing pain of grief almost brought her to her knees. She closed her eyes. Not one minute more would she waste.

"I'll keep your secret, Henry."

Max rotated her around to face him. "Wait, no, it's too risky. What if someone discovers he is still alive?"

"No one will. I will leave the country quietly. I will take off to South America." Henry turned to face Julien. "I will wait there until you can forgive me. I will wait with hope, until the end of my days."

Max shook his head. "But if you're not dead, she is still your wife."

"I am dead. Legally Livvy is my widow." Henry stepped forward and took hold of her hands. "Livvy, I am truly sorry for all of this last year. I did think I was doing the right thing for us all."

She stared into the familiar, oh so dear, brown eyes of her oldest friend. She nodded. "We must break all the rules for love."

A smile bloomed across Henry's face, and he bent to kiss her cheek. Then Henry crossed to where Julien sat. He went to his knees again and laid his head on Julien's lap. Julien looked across at her, and she quirked up one side of her mouth. He would have to make his own decision to forgive Henry. Julien's sigh was audible from across the room. Then he gently brushed his hand over Henry's hair.

Olivia turned back to Max. She placed a hand over his heart. "It doesn't matter the risks. Max, I love you beyond reason, beyond rules. I would risk anything to have you be mine. We can't get back the years that my father stole from us, but we can craft a new future together, a happy one. That will be the best revenge."

Max brushed the back of his fingers across her cheek. "Are you sure?"

"I know I have been cautious, and I have held back my feelings out of fear. But I refuse to waste even one more minute of my life denying how much you mean to me. Max, please, will you marry me, be mine for always?"

Max swept her up into his arms; her feet dangled several inches off the floor. He twirled her around in a dizzying circle. His laughter spilled into the room. Then he kissed her, soft and sweet. "Yes, my love. Yours for always and forever."

The End

Epilogue

One year later

OLIVIA STOOD BY the front window of the bookshop and watched a group of carolers sing outside of the tea shop next door. Their beautiful voices blended to sing "Oh Come All Ye Faithful." Foot traffic up and down High Street was brisk as people enjoyed the festival. She smiled as her husband's face appeared on the other side of the glass. He grinned and gave a wave. Olivia turned to the door as Max walked inside the shop.

"Happy Christmas Eve, Wife." He leaned down to kiss her.

"Happy Christmas Eve, Husband," she replied in kind.

"How was business this afternoon?"

"Busy. We sold all the Twelfth Night card decks and quite a few books." Olivia turned to the young woman sitting behind the desk. "Miss Martin, what does the tally say?"

"We sold twenty-two books today, six decks, and five stationary bundles." Her friendly brown eyes sparkled with excitement. "That's an all-time record for certain."

Miss Martin had become an invaluable employee. Sunny and personable, she was the polar opposite of the grouchy Mr. Buxley, and the town folk had taken notice. In the eight months Miss Martin had been working for Olivia, they had seen a steady increase in customers.

Last January, Mr. Buxley had taken his wife's advice, and the money Max had gotten from the sale of the contraband in the attic and retired. Olivia had offered a fair price for the building and its contents, and she believed that Mr. Buxley, despite his grumbling, was secretly happy to have the shop off his hands.

Olivia had altered her original plan to spend her days running the bookshop. She spent last winter implementing changes to the shop, and then she hired Miss Martin to run the day-to-day. She still loved to pop in and see how things were shaping up from time to time. But the past year had been filled with family and adventures of all types.

She and Max had married in February in an intimate ceremony in Marbury. Then they had spent springtime in London, introducing his sister into society. Olivia had found it easier now that she was older to navigate society functions. Perhaps it was partly because she found she did not care anymore what people were saying, and partly that she was incandescently happy being Max's wife.

During the summer, they had spent two months in the south of France with Louisa and his grandmother while Max's mother and Ginny had organized the relocation of their household from Paris to London. And this February, to celebrate their anniversary, she and Max were traveling to Italy. She was so excited; she could barely wait.

"Excellent," Max said. "I knew your idea to extend the Christmas market and create a town festival was brilliant."

Olivia raised an eyebrow. "Did you now?" He sure had grumbled quite a bit this month that the planning for the Christmas festival had taken up so much of her time.

"I am very proud of my very accomplished wife." Max wrapped her in his arms and kissed the tip of her nose. "Now, are you ready to go to Lucius's party?"

Lucius and Ellie were throwing a party to celebrate the anniversary of his business. They had invited the whole town to the brewery for the festivities. Olivia looked over her shoulder at Miss Martin.

"Go on. I'll close up and see you there in a bit." The woman made a shooing motion with her hands.

Max helped Olivia with her cape and ushered her outside to the waiting carriage. Once they were tucked inside, Max pulled her close. "Have I told you yet today that I love you?"

She snuggled close. "Not yet." She leaned up and kissed him. "I love you, too."

Not a day went by where they didn't appreciate the second chance they had been given. It had been hard to stay angry at Henry when he was the reason she had Max back in her life. "Oh, I almost forgot to tell you that we received a letter from Julien today."

"We did? I honestly never thought we would hear from them again after they sent word they had arrived safely in

Rio de Janeiro."

"He said they had settled in a lovely house by the ocean. The expedition is planned for next month, and he is brimming with excitement to start cataloging."

Max chuckled. "I always did think he was an odd duck for the way he enthused over plants. Good thing Henry is there to be the practical one and watch out for him."

"Yes, well, it's a good thing Henry is a fool for love." She squeezed her husband's hand.

Max bent and kissed the spot right underneath her ear that always sent shivers down her spine. "Hmmm, it's a good thing I am a fool for you."

Yes, it was. Olivia tipped her head so he could have better access to place kisses along her neck. She was forever grateful that this foolish man loved her. His persistence had not only renewed her Christmas spirit but renewed her faith in lasting love and happily-ever-afters.

Want more? Check out Charlotte and Daniel's story in *A Perfect Engagement*!

Join Tule Publishing's newsletter for more great reads and weekly deals!

If you enjoyed *Christmas at Belhaven Hall,*
you'll love the other books in...

The Maidens of Marbury series

Book 1: *A Perfect Engagement*

Book 2: *Saving a Scoundrel*

Book 3: *Christmas at Belhaven Hall*

Available now at your favorite online retailer!

About the Author

From the time she read fairytales as a child, Karla Kratovil was hooked on stories that ended in Happily Ever After. Now as an author of sexy historical romance she gets to craft her own happy endings. Karla lives right on the edge of Northern Virginia's wine country with her college sweetheart, two terrific teenagers, and two blond terriers. She is a Taurus. Like any good earth sign she loves good food, good wine, and getting her hands dirty growing things in her garden.

Thank you for reading

Christmas at Belhaven Hall

If you enjoyed this book, you can find more from all our great authors at TulePublishing.com, or from your favorite online retailer.

CPSIA information can be obtained
at www.ICGtesting.com
Printed in the USA
LVHW112138271022
731790LV00019B/409

Olivia's smile faltered. "Oh, well, my friends have promised to help me. So, I think I have it well in hand." She stared down intently into her teacup.

Her swift rejection of his offer to help stung, and he realized he'd missed the easy camaraderie they had in the past. Swallowing his disappointment, he sat back in the chair and stared into the fire. This house was technically his now, but he still felt like the boy who tagged along at holiday breaks. This was Henry's world, and Max felt like an interloper. Henry. Shit, the letter.

Max reached into his inner jacket pocket. "Livvy, I meant to give it to you this morning, but well, you didn't give me a chance."

"Give me what?" she replied.

"When I met with the solicitor, there was a sealed envelope left to me. Inside there were three letters from Henry. I'm sorry that this was not given to you immediately. Something about protocol." He offered her the letter he pulled from his pocket.

Olivia accepted it with a shaking hand. She laid it on her lap and ran her fingers across her name. "Thank you." She abruptly stood. "If you'll excuse me. I think I will retire to my room to read this."

He rose as well. "Of course. Wait, do you know who Julien is? The other two letters, one was for me and one for Julien, no last name."

"Yes, Julien is Mr. Galey. He was a good friend of Henry's. You can probably find him in the greenhouse. He is a